A Young Adult Psychological Mystery Thriller

BOOK #1

Emma Right

Dead Dreams, Book 1,

A contemporary young adult psychological thriller and suspense mystery.

Summary:

Eighteen-year-old Brie O'Mara has so much going for her: a loving family on the sidelines, an heiress for a roommate, and dreams that might just come true. Big dreams--of going to acting school, finishing college and making a name for herself. Eventually. What more could a girl hope for? Except her dreams are about to lead her down the road to nightmares. Nightmares that could turn into a deadly reality.

Watch the Dead Dreams by Emma Right trailer on www.youtube.com/user/YoungAdultAndKids/

Visit Emma at http://www.emmaright.com/blog or follow on Facebook.com/emma.right.author   and Facebook.com/DeadDreamsEmmaRight

or twitter follow @emmbeliever

This book is a work of fiction. Names, characters, places and incidents are either the product of the author's

imagination or are used fictitiously. Any resemblance to actual persons, living or dead, or to actual events or locales is entirely coincidental.

For information contact Right House at

http://www.emmaright.com

ISBN: 10:09892672-2-9

ISBN: 13:978-0-982672-2-9

ASIN: B00ESVEVBQ

Library of Congress Catalogue Number:2013914247

Version 2014.05.04 Editors: Dr. D. Hensley, Lisa Lickel

Book Cover Design: Lisa Hainline
@lionsgatebookdesign.com

Publisher Right House 2013

Printed in the United States of America

10 9 8 7 6 5 4 3 2 1

TO THE ONLY ONE WHO
CAN MAKE DREAMS
COME TRUE.

❖❖❖

"WHAT IF A MAN GAINS
THE WHOLE WORLD,
BUT
LOSES HIS SOUL?"

CONTENTS

DEDICATION

For Dreamers Everywhere.

❖Prologue❖

THEY SAY EACH DEAD body, a human corpse, has a scent all of its own, a sweet-sour smell. A cadaver dog picks up the odor as clearly as a mother recognizes a photo of her child. Of course, I wouldn't know, for I am no dog. I might as well have been, the way I'd stooped to yield to my basic instincts. My mind wandered to her, what her unique smell would be when, and if, they ever were to find her.

After what happened, I decided to write out the events that led to that day, and details, in case I'd missed something, or might need it for defense, or in case they found me dead. My relatives might need to piece together the things that had spiraled out of control, if they wanted to put me to rest, to forget me altogether. That would be least painful for them. I nodded to myself as I sat in the car. I thought of my most favorite girl in the world: Lilly. At least Lilly'd have my dog, Holly, and Rosco, my teddy, to remember me by.

My friends used to call me Brie, short for Brianna. But, I could hardly count anyone a friend any more. I'd have to resort to back-watching if I wanted to survive.

❖Chapter One❖

IT STARTED ON A WARM April afternoon. Gusts of wind blew against the oak tree right outside my kitchen balcony, in my tiny apartment in Atherton, California. Sometimes the branches that touched the side of the building made scraping noises. The yellow huckleberry flowers twining their way across my apartment balcony infused the air with sweetness.

My mother had insisted, as was her tendency on most things, I take the pot of wild huckleberry, her housewarming gift, to my new two-bedroom apartment. It wasn't really new, just new to me, as was the entire experience of living separately, away from my family, and the prospect of having a roommate, someone who could be a best friend, something I'd dreamed of since I finished high school and debuted into adulthood.

"Wait for me by the curb," my mother said, her voice blaring from the phone even though I didn't set her on speaker. "You need to eat better." Her usual punctuation at the end of her orders.

So, I skipped down three flights of steps and headed toward the side of the apartment building to await my mother's gift of the evening, salad in an á la chicken style, her insistent recipe to cure me of bad eating habits. At least it wasn't chicken soup double-boiled till the bones melted, I consoled myself.

I hadn't waited long when a vehicle careened round the corner. I heard it first, that high-pitched screech of brakes wearing thin when the driver rammed his foot against it. From the corner of my eye, even before I turned to face it, I saw the blue truck. It rounded the bend where Emerson Street met Ravenswood, tottered before it righted itself and headed straight at me.

I took three steps back, fell and scrambled to get back up as the vehicle like a giant bullet struck the sidewalk I had only seconds ago stood on. The driver must have lost control, but when he hit the sidewalk it slowed the vehicle enough so he could bridle his speed and manage the truck as he continued to careen down the street.

My mother arrived a half minute later but she had seen it all. Like superwoman, she leaped out of her twenty-year-old Mercedes and rushed toward me, all breathless and blonde hair disheveled.

"Are you all right?" She reached out to help me up.

"Yes, yes," I said, brushing the dirt off my yoga pants.

"Crazy driver. Brie, I just don't know about this business of you staying alone here like this." She walked back to her white Mercedes, leaned in the open window, and brought out a casserole dish piled high with something green. Make that several shades of green.

I followed her, admittedly winded."Seriously, Mom. It's just one of those things. Mad drivers could happen anywhere I live."

She gave me no end of grief as to what a bad idea it was for me to live alone like this even though she knew I was going to get a roommate.

"Mom, stop worrying," I said.

"You're asking me to stop being your mother, I hope you realize this."

"I'll find someone dependable by the end of the week, I promise." No way I was going back to live at home. Not that I came from a bad home environment. But I had my reasons.

I had advertised on Craig's List, despite my mother's protests that only scum would answer "those kinds of ads."

Perhaps there was some truth to Mother's biases, but I wouldn't exactly call Sarah McIntyre scum. If she was, what would that make me?

Sarah's father had inherited the family "coal" money. Their ancestors had emigrated from Scotland (where else, with a name like McIntyre, right?) in the early 1800s and bought an entire mountain (I kid you not) in West Virginia. It was a one-hit wonder in that the mountain hid a coal fortune under it, and hence the McIntyre Coal Rights Company was born. This was the McIntyre claim to wealth, and also a source of remorse and guilt for Sarah, for supposedly dozens of miners working for them had lost their lives due to the business, most to lung cancer or black lung, as it was commonly called. Hazards of the occupation.

And then there were cave-ins, which presented another set of drama altogether, Sarah said.

I sat across from her, the coffee table between us, in the small living room during our first meeting. "So, that's why you're not on talking terms with your family? Because of abuses of the coal company? " I asked.

We sipped hot cocoa and sat cross-legged in the crammed living room, which also doubled as the dining space. I'd never interviewed anyone before, although I'd read tips on the Internet.

"I just don't want to be reminded anymore," she said, twirling her dark ringlets round and round on her pointer finger.

"But, it's not entirely your dad's fault those people died of lung problems."

"I guess, but I just want to get away, you understand? Anyway, I'm almost twenty-one now. That's three years too late for moving out and establishing my own space." She took tiny sips of the cocoa, both hands cupping the mug as if she were cold.

I walked to the thermostat and upped the temperature. A slight draft still stole in from a gap in the balcony sliding door I always kept open a crack to let the air circulate.

"So, your family's okay with you living here? In California? In this apartment that's probably smaller than your bathroom? With a stranger?"

"First off, it's none of their business. Secondly, you and I won't *stay* strangers." Sarah flashed me a grin. "Besides, I'm tired of big houses with too many rooms to get lost in. And, have you lived in West Virginia?"

I shook my head. The farthest I'd been was Nevada when we went for our family annual ski vacation. "I heard it's pretty."

"If you like hot, humid summers and bitter cold winters. So, do I pass? As a roommate?"

She looked about at the ceiling. I wondered if she noticed the dark web in the corner and the lack of cornices and crown moldings. I was sure I smelled mold in the living room, too. But I wasn't in a position to choose. Sarah was.

"As long as you're not a psychopath and can pay rent." I returned her smile.

"I don't know about the psychopath part." She shrugged and displayed her white, evenly-spaced teeth. "But here's my bank account." She tossed me a navy blue booklet with gilded edges and with golden words "Bank of America" on the cover.

I fumbled as I caught it and was unsure what to do. "Should I peek?"

"Go on." She gestured, flicking her fingers at me as if I were a stray cat afraid to take a morsel of her offering.

"No secrets. I can well afford to pay rent. And, I'm a stable individual."

I flipped the first few pages and saw the numerous transactions in lumps my parents, who were by no means poor, would have gasped at. The last page registered the numbers: under deposits, $38,000. My eyes scanned the row of numbers and realized that the sum $38,000 came up every sixth of the month.

My mouth must have been open for she said, "You can stop gawking. It's only my trust fund. It comes to me regardless of where I am, or where I stay. So, do I make the cut?"

I handed the bank book back. We discussed the house rules: no smoking; no drugs, and that included pot; no boyfriend sleepovers or wild parties, which was a clause in my landlord's lease; and Sarah was to hand me her share of the rent, a mere $800, on the twenty-eighth of every month, since I was the main renter and she the sub-letter.

She didn't want anything down on paper—no checks, no contracts, and no way of tracing things back to her, she'd stressed a few times.

She fished in her Louis Vuitton and handed me a brown paper bag, the kind kids carry their school lunches in. I peeked inside and took out a stash of what looked like a wad of papers bundled together with a rubber band. Her three-month share of the deposit, a total of twenty-four crisp hundred-dollar bills. They had that distinct new-bank-notes-smell that spoke of luxury.

I gulped down my hot chocolate. "Why all the secrecy? I hope your parents will at least know your address." I said as I wrapped up the interview. I could understand not wanting her parents breathing down her neck, but as long as they didn't insist on posting a guard at the door, what was the harm of them knowing where she lived?

Sarah glanced about the room as if afraid the neighbors might have their ears pinned to the walls, listening.

She leaned forward and, her face expressionless, said softly, "My parents are dead."

❖Chapter Two❖

HAVING DECEASED PARENTS at such a young age could have explained Sarah's odd behavior. I sat up straight, and the hair at the back of my neck prickled, without my knowing exactly why.

"I'm sorry." I felt the blood draining from my face. Perhaps it was the thought of losing one's parents that shocked me.

"Oh, don't be," she said, almost flippantly. "They've been dead awhile. They had me in their forties, and Dad died of cancer. Lung cancer. Too much smoking. Ironic, isn't it? Mom just wilted after that and followed suit six months after."

She didn't seem in the least bit affected..

"So, who is it you're running from?"

"I just don't want my brother to know where I live."

I could already see the problems that could arise. My mom would, at this point, have waved a red flag and shouted, "There, Brie. Bad brother. Bad blood. Do you want to be dragged into this?

Who knows what crimes the brother might have been involved in?"

Of course, Mom leaned toward melodramatics and I am my own person now. I would like to think I could make sound decisions. Besides, something about Sarah intrigued me. It wasn't just her transparency with me, or her globs of money, although I could see how it'd be fun to hang out with someone with her bounty and who didn't seem caught up.

"So what's with your brother? He's jealous of your inheritance?" *And what about troublesome cousins?*

"Not inheritance." She rolled her eyes as if I'd made a ridiculous mistake and had said two plus two was five. "Trust fund. The inheritance kicks in only when I turn twenty-one, which is in a few weeks, and I keep a clean record—no arrests, no misdemeanors.

"Todd, my brother, receives his own funds. Same deal as me. Grandpa was fair that way. Anyway, my dad was Grandpa Luke's only child from his first marriage. Both Todd and I get the inheritance from my dad's estate at the same time, after *my* twenty-first birthday. Provided…"

She looked at me quizzically, almost sizing me up.

I found myself gripping the edge of the coffee table and leaned forward. "Provided?"

"Like I said, provided we never get into trouble or make a nuisance of ourselves with the law or lead a life he deemed irresponsible. Grandpa was particular that way. He saw too many rich kids become a pain to society. So, my brother and I must show a clean slate. Prove we're worthy of the inheritance."

"I see." I didn't, really. Who did she have to prove this to? How many others had rejected Sarah's apartment-sharing application based on her secrecy conditions and far-from-common background? But still, she had the dough and I was desperate to seal the deal. Two others who'd inquired about the apartment had sounded high, speaking with a melodic tone indicative of their "happy" state, and a third had never called back even after profusely promising to. I couldn't afford a flaky roommate.

Running to my parents to bail me out each time a housemate wriggled out of a deal wasn't an option and I didn't make enough to bear the rent alone. Just as long as Sarah paid her share, and didn't try to murder me in my sleep, that was all I expected out of this arrangement.

"What happens to the inheritance if one of you goofs up or breaks the law?" I asked.

"The one left standing will gain the other's share. And, I can tell you, the sum would make Captain Cook rouse from his grave." She made a spooky gesture with her arms, as if she were a ghost.

"And you're staying away from your brother, because...?"

She drained the last of the cocoa and smacked her lips. "Because Todd's waiting for me to slip up. Did I also mention that if one of us perishes, the other gains the inheritance, too?"

"I would've recalled that detail." And what an incentive to do away your sibling.

"So?" Her brown eyes widened, and she jerked her chin at me. "Am I acceptable? You won't be sorry. You can keep the deposit now."

At this point, I should have asked why *I* made the cut. Sarah could surely rent a place five times the size of this dump. Okay, the place wasn't a dump, and the apartment was in a safe neighborhood in the woodsy town of Atherton, mostly mansions with large parcels in the most affluent part of the San Francisco Bay Area. Like most cities in the Northern California suburbs, Atherton deemed it good manners to apportion a corner of its ritzy acreage to middle-income dwellers—or as in my case, subterranean-income-level dwellers.

My parents had insisted on a respectable neighborhood if their darling daughter had to succumb to apartment living. When the Sky Atherton Apartments came on the market, they'd insisted I apply. Never mind it was about a thousand dollars more than my budget allowed. But, I was on an agenda to prove something to myself, and to them, and I didn't have a choice. People had called me "coddled," as though I were an egg, or "sheltered." I wanted to escape these stigmas.

I studied Sarah as she raised her eyebrows. She looked sober. She had money. She seemed like a clean-cut, girl-next-door type, and except for her relations who she shouldn't be blamed for, I couldn't see a reason to refuse.

So, Sarah moved into that nine-hundred-square- foot, third-story apartment that very afternoon. She didn't bring much furniture, just an antique-white twin bed with matching bedside table and dresser. She also had two hefty Louis Vuitton suitcases and two cartons, one measuring about four-by-four feet and another that was humongous and could have easily hidden a small elephant, especially the way it weighed. She refused my offers to help move it and struggled as she heaved and pushed it into her bedroom.

"Why not hire some professionals for this?" I asked as I got up to lend her a hand. *What's the point of having gobs of money?* It was a good thing I had on my usual yoga pants—I vacillated between them and skinny jeans. Sarah, on the other hand, tottered on five-inch heels and wiggled in a super-tight miniskirt.

She shook her head as if I'd proposed something preposterous. How had she even gotten it into her Jaguar, or gotten it from there and onto the dolly I'd borrowed from Mrs. Mott, my then-next door neighbor?

"The Jag's backseat folds down," she explained when I asked, as if this were common knowledge. "Mine is a special order. Besides, have you ever been in one?"

I got the message.

Her other three pieces of furniture arrived late in the evening via a white-glove delivery service. She gave the delivery man a hundred-dollar bill each—gratuity, she'd said. I should have insisted on helping with removing the cardboard cartons and gotten a tip, too.

Later, I heard Sarah through her closed door, heaving and puffing over something in her room. I walked to it, placed my ear by the door jamb, and wondered what secret she kept in that heavy carton.

Mother called that night to find out who I'd settled on for a new roommate. I never mentioned I'd only had one viable candidate, and I didn't specify details, either— just that I'd found someone not on drugs. "Nor on pot." Mother was specific about using the word "pot," just in case some junkie, or worse, Libertarian, didn't consider pot a type of drug.

"How can you decide so quickly to take her in?" Mother seemed disturbed and spoke with a shrill voice, as was her practice when she felt thus. "Did you even run a credit check?"

I gave her a brief history of the McIntyre fortune, and that pacified her for the moment.

The next few days, Mother called again and again, asking to meet Sarah, but Sarah kept making excuses. Once, she claimed she was late for a show, a matinee to a ballet in the city. Then, another day, she insisted the brakes on her brand-new, forest-green Jaguar XK coupe, no less, needed servicing. She even, by way of excuse, said her dry cleaning was messed up.

"But, can't you even have coffee with her, *once*?" I asked Sarah one rare evening when I didn't have work and we were watching an oldie movie and crunching on microwaveable popcorn— the kind they'd recently confirmed could be carcinogenic.

With her mouth full she just waved at me as though I were a mosquito and pointed to the TV: her signal to shut up and watch the screen.

As the days passed, my ears should have perked up at the warning signs, the excuses that bordered on lies, but still, I could see why someone would be wary about meeting her roommate's parents, especially if the parents were anything like mine and had their noses in places even a dog wouldn't think of sniffing. I, myself, would have run away from them, given the chance.

Besides, I was juggling two jobs: a receptionist at Stay Fit in the wee hours of the morning, and a Starbucks barista in the afternoon. Thus my mind wasn't always sharp, even with all the free caffeine. I never suspected Sarah wanted to avoid meeting my parents, my friends, co-workers, or, for that matter, Mrs. Mott, the only neighbor I was on talking terms with.

"Mrs. Mott could really do with some help," I said, one afternoon, while balancing a half-dozen cardboard cartons and heading toward the little old lady's apartment next door. She seemed frail and had her doctor with her.

"I'm busy," Sarah said, applying a deep copper hue to her French-tipped toenails.

"It's too bad you won't meet her. She used to be a concert pianist in her younger days. She's a neat lady."

"I have a doctor's appointment," she said without looking up.

"Are you sick?"

"Just routine stuff. Maybe I can meet her another day

I stared at Sarah. "She's moving to a senior home. She had a heart attack yesterday. There won't be another day." And I stalked out the door.

❖ Chapter Three ❖

MRS. MOTT HAD MORE CLOTHES than I'd ever imagined a lady in her seventies would possess. She must have not gotten rid of anything since she was twenty. I had volunteered to box them all for her—without first finding out what I'd signed myself up for.

When I was downstairs, stuffing the cartons in the rented U-Haul that would take Mrs. Mott's clothes to her new residence, a siren chirped once, as if asking why the moving truck was blocking its way. Two police cruisers drove up and stopped right behind it. I looked at the curb to see if the truck was parked illegally.

Two cops stepped out of each of the Impala cruisers and headed toward me. I'd never had any trouble with the law, not even a speeding ticket, but still I was nervous about the four officers trudging toward me, each with one hand on a holster. With their grim faces, they looked like they were only too keen to use me as target practice if I so much as dropped a candy wrapper by accident. So, I spun around and skipped back toward the apartment.

"Hey, Miss, wait up!" the lady cop hollered. She had her blonde hair scooped up in a tight ponytail. I had never achieved this no-wisp look, even when I had my hair gelled during my ballet-bun days.

I stopped in my tracks and told myself there was nothing to be worried about. "Yes?" I faced them as they now stood, shoulder-to-shoulder behind me. Fast walkers.

"Do you live in there?" the lady officer, Sergeant. Charlene Twist, asked. She pointed to the entrance to my apartment building.

I nodded. "What's up?"

"Do you know a Mrs. Marcia Mott?"

I didn't know Mrs. Mott's first name, so I just stared dumbly at her. "Why? What's wrong?"

"Do you know her? She's about seventy-five."

"If you mean my next-door neighbor, sure. She's moving out. But I can't chat. I actually took a couple hours emergency leave to help her move her stuff." I jerked my head toward the U-Haul truck.

"Has the ambulance been here?"

"They're coming soon. But it's not because she's gotten worse, right? It's just that she can't sit up."

"No need to worry your pretty head over this," the male cop said. "We just have a few questions."

"Mrs. Mott's doctor's in the apartment with her. He can probably answer you about her condition."

"It's not her condition we're worried about. Her son wanted us to check on things."

Sorry I asked. "What do you want to know?"

"Mr. Mott said his mother thought she saw someone prowling a couple of days back and that gave her a scare. We don't know how this is related to her present condition, but we need to ask neighbors if they saw anything suspicious."

"Prowling? Where?"

"That's what we're hoping to verify. She hasn't been cogent in her details. It might be nothing."

"I can't say I noticed anything suspicious." I'd had that dream and thought I'd seen a m a n ' s face peering at me from outside my bedroom window at three in the morning a couple nights back. But I wasn't the sort to pay much attention to dreams. Also, my imagination tended to get wild, especially when I lacked sleep. Besides, we were on the third floor, and I seriously doubted anyone would want to rob anything I had. In any case, when I'd rubbed my eyes, the face disappeared.

"If you recall anything concrete, call me." The lady cop handed me a business card. I slipped it into my jeans pocket.

❖ Chapter Four ❖

THAT EVENING, SARAH came home with a patch on her arm. I thought she looked pale.

"What happened?" I asked, pointing at the tape on the inside of her wrist.

"Had to get to the doctor's again. Just a blood test."

"You're not super sick, are you?" Thoughts of cancer ran through my mind. My dad was a doctor and always brought home horror stories. "Have you been having hot flashes?"

"Do I look menopausal?"

"Hot flashes—that's one of the symptoms of cancer. I saw you shivering the first day you came here. At the interview."

She barked out a laugh. "Don't be silly. I'm healthy as a horse. What did the cops want?"

"The ones I met downstairs earlier?"

"Did you speak with any others?"

"No. Mrs. Mott thought she saw prowlers. They just want to see if I noticed anything out of the ordinary."

"Just keep me out of it, whatever it is." She slunk to her bedroom, but before she slammed the door, I hollered after her.

"Don't worry, the US government isn't after you." Paranoia runs in her veins, I mumbled to myself. But still, I was worried for her. If she was ill, with some blood disease or something horrible, would she tell me?

Sarah glared at me as she turned and closed the door.

Later that night, as we wolfed down some sushi takeout, I persisted with the same meet-my-friends theme. "You should hang out with some of them." Not that I had too many chums to boast of, or had the luxury to socialize much with time being my enemy. "If you're going to make the Bay Area your home, it can't hurt to meet new people around here."

"I have enough friends."

Really? Who? I was going to ask, but didn't.

❖Chapter Five❖

So, Sarah stayed a loner, even refusing my attempt to include her when I asked her out for ice cream with my co-workers one rare afternoon. Only once did she accept my invitation to work out as my guest at Stay Fit. She came to exercise but forgot her gear and had to borrow my yellow sweats.

One of my co-workers, Susan Summers, saw her in passing, mistook her for me, and complained to Thao that I'd gone Zumba-ing during my official hours. Even Peter came to Susan's defense saying we looked alike, so it was an understandable error.

But after that, Sarah never wanted to step inside Stay Fit.

At least we got to spend some girl time there when I had a fifteen-minute break. She probed about my lost love, Drew, a topic I'd rather not dwell on. On our way home in my second-hand Mini Cooper, a black-top with a faded green bottom half—it was a graduation gift my parents had insisted upon—Sarah said, "I'm sorry about Mrs. Mott."

I'd overheard two other neighbors whispering in the lobby about how Mrs. Mott passed away. She'd seemed so healthy when I'd met her a month back. Seventy-five is a ripe age, and the heart attack must have weakened her. But still.

"Me, too. I'm going to miss her."

"How'd she die?"

"Another heart attack. The cops came again and asked about loiterers."

"What did you tell them?" she asked.

"I didn't see any. Did you?"

She shrugged, looking almost sad.

"That's the thing with the heart. You can never tell its condition till it's too late."

That was probably the most profound thing Sarah had ever shared with me.

❖Chapter Six❖

THE FIRST NIGHT THE BURGLAR broke into our home, I was wiped out and completely wasted. That morning, Susan Summers at Stay Fit had called in sick last-minute, and I had to add two hours to my unearthly dawn shift. After that I couldn't even grab lunch since I had to scoot to Starbucks, driving like a mad duck in my Mini Cooper. Friday afternoon was an especially busy time for Starbucks. Forget about grabbing a minute to down a latte or two to keep my eyelids from drooping.

The moment I got home at eight, I stuffed my mouth with leftover pepperoni pizza, cold from the refrigerator, and practically crawled to the shower before hitting the sack. A bag of potatoes would have looked more awake than I did.

"Brie, wake up," Sarah whispered as she shook my arm vigorously.

25

Who is she afraid of waking with all that whispering? I was the only one in the bedroom. I glanced at my bedside clock. The green light of the digital claimed it was three-ten. Or, I should say, *already* three-ten, since I always dragged my body out of bed at four-thirty to brace myself for Stay Fit.

Then, even in the dimness, I noticed Sarah's eyes were glistening. "What's wrong?" Was she ill after all?

"Shhh! They could still be here."

"They? Who?"

"Shhh! Them, they, he…." She broke off, sobbing.

I turned on the bedside lamp, and she struggled, intending to stop me. I jerked back when I saw her face. Blood dripped from one side of her head.

"My God! Sarah!" I exclaimed, even though I wasn't the believing-in-God type. My parents were to be blamed for my aversion to God. Too many inconsistencies and unanswered questions.

"What happened?" Her eyes, wild, looking about like a frightened deer caught in a headlight, welled up with tears.

"They're—he's after me. He's going to kill me."

"Who?" I jumped to my feet and rushed to the door. Thank goodness she'd shut it. I placed my ear to the doorjamb and listened. Were the burglars still outside?

Sarah sobbed uncontrollably. Too loudly.

"Shh! Sarah, are they still here?" I shook her in a vain attempt to keep her calm.

"Just one man. I don't know. I rammed the door into his face when he dragged me by the hair." She rubbed at a spot on her scalp. "I think he left, maybe."

"We have to call the cops."

"No, no, please. You can't." She pulled my arm when I reached for my yellow duffel by the foot of my bed, where my cell phone lay.

"We mustn't. You don't get it. Todd!" She said under her breath.

Todd? This was no ordinary sibling rivalry. This was beyond me. Sarah was hiding something. What if she was a new release from a mental ward? How could I have confirmed she was sane and not suffering from schizophrenia?

My mind lingered on the patch on her arm. Was she really who she said she was? Was she seriously ill---in the head? It was just as well that she paid everything in cash. And Todd, her brother...how was he involved? What was he? Some hit man?

My mother would be livid if she knew about tonight. She might even force me to return home, bar my bedroom windows in that house of hers. Rapunzel would have stood a better chance of escaping her tower.

Perhaps it'd be better if we didn't go to the cops. Things had a way of leaking back to my parents.

"We don't know if your brother had anything to do with this. Could just be a burglar," I said. I rummaged inside the duffel for my phone, but this time Sarah yanked the bag out of my grasp and tossed it onto the bed.

"No cops! Which burglar would want to target us when there are those estate homes around?" She flicked her hand at the window and waved it about.

Good point. "Maybe the burglars know we don't have an alarm system. Those big homes are armed to the hilt with serious stuff. It's easier to rob the Pentagon." Still, we were three stories up. It wasn't as if our apartment was that easy to get to, either.

Sarah bit her lower lip, her frown deepening. "I'll buy an alarm tomorrow. Later today. I meant to anyway."

"Why would you even think your brother would want to hurt you?"

"Duh! My inheritance? And my trust fund?" She wiped her eyes with the back of her hand.

"Maybe you should move out, Sarah. Find a safer, or I should say, better-guarded place. Like the Pentagon."

Her eyes widened, and suddenly I saw a frightened little girl staring at me.

"How could you say that? Joking at a time like this?" Her chin quivered the way my little sister Lilly's would when she felt sorry about something.

I pressed my ear to the bedroom door again. "I'm going to check and see if anyone's still out there." I thought of asking Mrs. Mott for help but remembered her death.

"Wait!" Sarah rushed toward me and brought a hand out from under her green sweatshirt. She pointed a gun at me.

"Sarah!"

"I know how to operate this. It's a Glock. And I have a license. All legit."

"Don't point that thing at me."

❖Chapter Seven❖

"**THERE'S A SAFETY CATCH**. See?" Sarah pointed to the Glock.

No, I didn't see. Big consolation, that safety gadget. "I don't trust safety catches. Or guns." Or you, I wanted to say. I went to unlock the door, but Sarah stepped closer toward me, the Glock still aimed at my chest.

"Could we please set that gun on the edge, over there?" I pointed to the corner of the bed farthest from me. I used the voice I'd always practiced on my dog, Holly, when I wanted to sound firm.

"But, we might need it."

"Why didn't you use it on the thug?"

"He was too fast. I always hide it under my mattress. By the time I hit him and rushed to the bed to get it, he'd run to the kitchen. Then, I couldn't hear him."

"So, he's probably gone. We should look around and see what's missing." I jerked my chin at the Glock. "That baby stays on my bed." If Sarah had made it safely to my room without any more attacks, the burglar was probably gone. Besides, I didn't trust her waving that weapon around. Surely it was safer with the intruder than with Sarah and her gun.

We tiptoed across the hallway and except for the wind whistling through a crack in one of the windows, sounding like a banshee, the apartment was quiet as a graveyard.

"He must have cut the window with a glass cutter after climbing up the balcony," Sarah whispered, even though we'd agreed no one was there.

Perhaps my potted honeysuckle, my mother's housewarming gift that had grown wild, had provided him with a good hold as he'd hauled himself up to our third-floor balcony. We stood still in the kitchen and strained our ears, but only the sound of the oak branch scraping the side of the building near the kitchen window disturbed the quiet of the night. He'd left no visible prints, no markings, nothing we could see.

"Let's hope he left some DNA stuff," I said. She looked blankly at me. How could I get her to see we needed to bring the cops in on this? I was willing to risk my mother finding out if our lives were at stake.

"Let's check out your room," I said, trying to sound brave.

Sarah gripped my arm, but I walked ahead of her.

Four of the drawers in Sarah's bedroom were pulled clear off the dresser and were stacked in a tower on the floor. Except for a massive writing desk, the matching set of dresser with the drawers, and her white four-poster twin bed, she'd kept her room decor to a minimum. We rummaged through the stacked drawers.

"You didn't hear him do this?" I motioned at the tottering stack.

She shook her head. "My Rolex watch is missing," she said after a while.

"Anything else?" That's pretty paltry loot considering all the bother to break in.

She shrugged and led me to her closet.

"What's that?" I pointed to a huge black box hidden behind her cocktail-looking dresses, some long, some with flirty frills and most terribly short.

She pushed the dresses aside, knelt before the black box, and placed one hand on a knob. "My safe."

So, *that* was what had lain in that humongous carton. Was the burglar after her treasure chest?

She twisted the safe's knob, and after a few turns left and right and a click, she heaved the door open. One by one she removed velvet-covered boxes and opened them. One held fine jewelry, her mother's diamond earrings, an heirloom from her Scottish great- grandmother, she said. In another lay a Mikimoto pearl necklace. She set these boxed treasures, which totaled about a dozen, by her foot after she checked their contents. She had numerous papers hidden in the safe, too. Most of them were rolled up like scrolls.

"What's with all those in there?" I asked as I peeked over her shoulder and pointed at the trash. *Don't tell me she litters in her own safe!*

We'd always bickered about her lack of housekeeping standards. She left a trail of mess in her wake and tossed all sorts of paperwork everywhere: grocery receipts stuffed in kitchen drawers, ice cream wrappers on counters and tables. It was a pain picking up the pieces, literally. It must have been a headache for the maids who had to clean up after her in that huge West Virginian mansion she grew up in. But, things have a way of working out. Later, it was in her trash that I would discover answers that prevented me from running into the arms of my deceiver.

Sarah took out one of the scrolls and unrolled it. "Gawd! You never saw stock certificates before? Birthday presents from my dad, since I was two. They're old. Coca- Cola, Apple. Oracle. The bluest of blue chips in here."

I couldn't imagine any toddler being thrilled at getting stock documents as presents. For the first time I noticed the safe was plugged into the wall socket and had a temperature control. Refrigerated? Sarah and her advance technology.

"Why's your safe plugged in?" I knew nothing about safes. Some other closed boxes were arranged in the back.

"Humidity control."

"We can't ignore this burglary, Sarah. We have to tell someone. What if we get killed next time this thug breaks in?" Where had I placed Sergeant Twist's card? It had probably gotten tattered in the wash, if it was still in my yoga pants.

"No! You don't understand. You can't trust anyone. My brother's well-connected."

"We need to know if this is really your brother after you. The law's here to protect you. Besides, didn't you say if Todd's caught in illegal or criminal actions, he'd lose his trust fund? And inheritance? That might take him off your back, if we have evidence that could nail him."

Sarah searched inside one of the drawers on the floor. She brought out a dark green book, only about two inches wide by three inches long.

"He didn't get this." She tapped it on her palm.

My face must have shown confusion.

"I keep tabs of all the places Todd's been. Every trip he's taken and dates."

"Why?"

"Some of the places he frequents every two, three weeks. At least that's what my informers reported. I think he has a girlfriend there, or someone special." Her eyes flitted to the ground as if this news pained her somehow.

"So, you hired a P. I. to track him? Perfect! We'll hire the same guy to sleuth for us."

"We can't," she said rather sharply.

My eyes glanced at the bedside clock on the dresser. Almost four thirty. *I have to be up already. Bummer.* "Why can't we hire your P. I.?"

"He's disappeared. I tried to get a hold of Jackson— that's his name—after I saw your Craig's List ad, and don't get mad at this, but I wanted to run a background check on you to be sure you're a nobody so my brother or anyone else can't find me. But Jackson's secretary said he hadn't reported to work for two weeks, and they didn't know where he was. Not like him to just up and leave."

So, she'd tried to do a background check on me. I should have played the same game with her. At least I would have landed with a saner roommate. I thought of Peter Salazar. His brother was a cop but worked as a P. I. now. "I have to get ready for work. Pete Salazar can help."

"Pete Salazar?"

"The guy at Stay Fit."

"Ah, the guy who hangs onto your every word."

"He does not."

"I saw him gawk at you the day I was there."

"That's because he mistook you for me, and he was trying to see how alike we looked."

She rolled her eyes and shook her head. "You're so blind. Can't you see he's all eyes on you?"

It wasn't that Pete wasn't cute, what with his shaggy blond hair and deep-set eyes, but ever since my high school sweetheart, Drew, had disappeared to New York and taken my heart with him, this bitter taste in my mouth always came up when my mind wandered to the *idea* of another boyfriend. Maybe I was one of those destined to be single forever. Like a nun. "Your imagination needs some reining in. Anyway, Pete's brother can help. He's a P.I."

"You should go out with Peter some time. Or, are you still hung up on that rich little boy who ditched you in high school?"

How'd she know I was thinking of Drew? *My face must be such an open book.*

"He didn't ditch me." That was what I'd convinced myself. "Do you want to find out who just broke into our place, or not?" I glared at her.

Sarah wrung her hands as though they were wet rags. "Don't say anything about my family's history, or that it could be my brother doing this, okay? If word leaks out, Todd could press charges on me for trying to soil his good name. Slander, or something. It could back fire."

"I'll be discrete. But you'd better not stay home alone today."

"I'll take my laptop and go to the library. I can research on a good alarm company. One with video and sound capture."

Growing up rich sure kept her abreast of technology and security systems.

"Call my cell when you want to come back here." The hair on my arms stood when I recalled

Sarah's frightened eyes. "Better clean up that blood on your forehead. How'd you get it, anyway?'

She strode to the doorway, ran her finger on the edge of the door, and displayed the blood on her finger. The burglar must have slammed her head on the edge of the door when he'd tried to drag her out.

But, what had he been trying to do? Besides robbing her? If he'd wanted her dead, he wouldn't have bothered to get her out of the room. And he'd only stolen her Rolex. And what was that worth? Ten thousand, max? Was it just a warning?

Sarah might not have been telling me everything. She always locked her bedroom door, too. So had she forgotten to lock it last night? Maybe the burglar had the key, but how was that possible? Only Mr. Yamamoto, our landlord, kept the spare ones.

"Sarah, which of your friends have you spoken to since you moved in?" It had only been three weeks. Maybe a snake was disguised as a buddy? Todd could have spun a yarn and offered a reward for Sarah's whereabouts, especially since his upside amounted to quite a treasure.

"Only Ken and Kaleb—the K brothers, I call them. Oh, and Megan. I've known her since forever, all the way back in kindergarten in West Virginia. I hooked up with her a few months back. She wouldn't have told Todd. She hates him. Even threw up on his head once when we were kids." She narrowed her eyes. "And you, of course. *You* know I'm here."

I let that slide. "And my parents," I added. *Let's see what she'll still say to that.*

"The K brothers have never met Todd. They work at Bank of America, and I got to know them, maybe a few months back. They're typical banker types. Clean-cut and do everything above board. Hardly burglar material."

Back in my room, my alarm clock rang so I excused myself after arranging to meet Sarah back at the apartment during my lunch break. The security people could install the system, then. I didn't ask how she was going to get them here on such short notice that very afternoon; cash could buy quite a few favors. I'd have to let my landlord know, convince Mr. Yamamoto an alarm would raise his apartment's value. He, too, could be swayed by the US currency.

❖Chapter Eight❖

I BUMPED INTO PETER Salazar as I flung my gym bag behind the front desk counter. I hoped I could exercise a bit before I had to leave for home and then my Starbucks stint. *Might help to pump some adrenaline into my system and keep me awake.*

"Hey, Pete. Got a sec?" I motioned for him to get behind the counter so no patron could overhear me.

Pete's eyes widened when I told him. Of course, I skipped Sarah's personal details. He stepped forward and petted my shoulder as if I were a puppy.

"Sure you're going to be okay tonight? I could camp out in your living room." He barked a short laugh, but his eyes spoke a concern I'd never seen before. *Sarah could be right.* He might have liked me more than I cared to admit. That could be a bummer, since he made such an awesome friend. Why spoil something with a relationship? Perhaps if Drew and I had only stayed friends, his parents might have allowed us to keep in touch.

"We're thinking of hiring someone to guard our

apartment. At least till we feel comfortable with the security system Sarah's getting." I broached the subject of his brother, Jim. His half-brother, different moms, same dad, Pete clarified.

Sarah had agreed to a blank check, perhaps even having two persons back-to-back, I told Peter. "Maybe your brother could see if he could get burglar's prints off the door. I think I know which window the thug came through. But, I'm no Nancy Drew."

"I'll call Jim, but he'd want to know what we're dealing with." Pete was smarter than he looked. He was tall and brawny, with a permanent tan some of us girls at Stay Fit tended to make fun of, but still, he was pleasant to be around. "What with Jim's cop background, he can be very suspicious," he continued.

I'd sworn to Sarah not to mention her fortune. "He's not going to say anything to his old cop friends, right?"

"Jim didn't exactly retire on good terms with his department, so he's not going to tell them much. He's discreet."

"I appreciate it, Pete." I tiptoed and pecked him on the cheek. He went as red as a fire truck.

"If you have to go, go. I'll cover for you," Pete said as he handed me Jim's number. "Jim's wife left him a decade back, and so he had to raise his only son by himself. He might be busy, but tell him you're my friend and he'll make time for you."

Later, Jim called me back and agreed to meet at the apartment. He'd get there during my lunch break, a few minutes before my scheduled time with Sarah. I would return to Stay Fit later to finish my shift and repay Pete for the hours he'd covered for me.

I told Jim to call me when he got there so I could open the door. Sure wouldn't want to let the burglar in by mistake. When I neared home, all sorts of scenes played out in my head.

As I inserted the key into the lock at the front door, the thought that someone might be inside waiting with an axe crossed my mind. Too many horror movies in my high school years. However, all seemed calm inside the apartment. Sarah wasn't home yet. I walked to the kitchen and looked out the window. An idea struck me.

I slipped on my leather gloves and sneaked into Sarah's bedroom. We'd agreed she should leave her door unlocked(a rarer-than-a-blue-moon occurrence) and her room undisturbed so the P.I. could take pictures. Of course, she hadn't known I was coming home earlier than our planned noon appointment, as I'd forfeited my exercise routine.

What else was the burglar after, besides Sarah's Rolex?

I rummaged through her clothes in the stacked drawers. The dark green notebook was gone from the topmost bin—probably still in her LV. But, under her lacy underwear, a card poked through. Probably it had slipped out of the notebook.

It was plain except for the name and telephone number scripted on one side: "Jackson Anderson. 650- 500-7456."

Her sleuth. The missing P.I. Sarah'd mentioned. I didn't find anything else except for a bunch of old receipts from an assortment of high-fashion stores. I slipped the card into my jeans pocket. It wouldn't do to use my cell, as it was traceable. I doubted public phones even existed these days, so using that was out of the question. Could a call via Skype be traced back to me? Maybe via an I.P. Address? I would have to figure how to call Jackson and still conceal my identity.

A quick check in the trash in Sarah's bathroom revealed she had receipts she'd torn into two and three pieces each. Most were bills from Nordstrom and a Patek Philippe boutique. I hadn't noticed her new purchase. Patek Philippe was more than just a high-end watch. It represented a statement for the rich and snooty. *Who wears watches these days?* Short of cooking dinner, my cell phone, a Samsung Galaxy S5, could do just about everything from telling time to reminding me of appointments, and it cost less than a tenth of a Patek Philippe.

I stuffed the torn receipts into my jeans pocket without being exactly certain why. Maybe Jim would have ideas Sarah wouldn't think to connect. I ran through the possibility in my mind.

Maybe the burglar followed her after stalking

her at the Patek Philippe store. Hoping to rob her sooner, he never had a chance, so he'd stalked her home instead, and had to make-do with the Rolex.

Had it been a burglar's face I'd seen by the window that night Mrs. Mott had suffered the heart attack? I'd dismissed the apparition as a figment of my imagination, but what if it was what had scared Mrs. Mott in the first place?

I traced the timeline and felt Mrs. Mott had the scare and subsequent heart attack a week back. I took the watch receipt out and looked for the date of purchase at the bottom, but it wasn't there. It was torn off. Assuming Mrs. Mott had spotted the burglar that evening, had he been checking to see if I were the girl to rob? But, it was dark, and no way could he have identified either of us from the window.

Still, something bugged me, though I couldn't pinpoint what it was. I went to the kitchen and made myself a PBJ sandwich. My mother would flip if she knew I hadn't been religious about eating salad as she'd regimented at home.

❖Chapter Nine❖

JIM SALAZAR ARRIVED five minutes later. He looked about fifty, at least to my eighteen-year-old eyes. And paunchy, as if he'd had too much beer all his life. What with his receding hairline kept hidden under a red Forty-Niners baseball cap, he didn't look anything like Pete, who must have been about two decades younger.

I couldn't imagine him a cop. How had he chased down agile criminals? Yet, he seemed meticulous in his work.

He dusted the doorjamb and the windowsill with a thin brush he'd pulled out of a fat silver briefcase with dents in its corners. The burglar must have climbed up to the balcony, Jim said. He pointed to an oak branch that almost touched Mrs. Mott's former kitchen window.

"Your burglar's one observant bloke. He must be a pro at this sort of thing." Jim said.

"Bloke." What an English word. I nodded. Maybe the bloke wasn't a random stalker intent on robbing Sarah, after all. What if he was hired?

Jim explained that instead of using the sliding door, the perpetrator had climbed onto the ledge and crept in through the window I always kept slightly open to let air circulate. Jim also took pictures of the safe and the crumpled comforter on the bed, when I told him Sarah hadn't gotten back to sleep after. He scoured the surface with a penknife-looking flashlight. It felt like watching a CSI episode in slow motion.

"So, any clues?" I squinted at the messy bed sheet.

"Don't touch anything yet," he said. "We don't want to contaminate."

I pressed my thumb into my pocket as I remembered the torn receipts and how I might have already compromised the crime scene. Jim wouldn't be happy if I told.

"See here?" He tweezed out a thin, dark brown hair, short and straight, and showed it to me. "Sarah's?"

I shook my head. "She's dark red, and curly. And, as you can see...." I twirled my straight mousey brown tresses in front of my face. "I'm too light to be its owner, either."

It was true Peter had seen the subtle similarities in our features and the shape of our faces. (Maybe Pete had been scrutinizing me more than I cared to admit.) But our coloring was dissimilar and at a glance a random stranger meeting us on the street may not have thought we looked alike at all especially since Sarah wore heavier make-up.

Jim asked, "Does she bring boyfriends here?"

I shook my head. "It's in our contract. Our landlord specifically stated no wild parties, and so I translated that as no guys overnight. She may have a boyfriend, but she's never mentioned him."

"We don't have much to go on. I got a partial print by the sill, but it could have been one of you girls. Hundreds of prints all over the furniture. I'd need to run the partial print. Do you mind if I get some of my contacts to take a look? I'd need your fingerprints, as well as Sarah's."

"Yeah, but don't tell Sarah. She's paranoid about privacy. Very into conspiracy theory. Thinks the government may be after her." I looked about the room and noticed an empty drinking glass on the desk. "Bet you can get her prints off that." I pointed at the Waterford crystal goblet from her personal collection, which she always set next to her bedside table.

Jim gingerly bagged it. "Expensive taste. Sure she won't miss it?"

"She has a dozen. Make sure you don't tell her, though, or anyone else about the prints. Just in case word leaks out. In fact, if you can destroy the prints leading back to us *after* you've used them, it'd be best. She likes to keep her identity secret. Plight of the rich in the first world." I felt obligated to inform him of the McIntyre wealth, and Jim raised his eyebrows more than once and nodded knowingly.

"And you still think your parents shouldn't hear about this?" He raised his eyebrows again.

"You don't know my parents. Finger-in-every-pot sorts of people."

Jim held his palm out as if to say, "I get it." He scrunched his mouth and said, "So, only a stolen Rolex?"

I briefed him on my theory about the possibility of the stalker zeroing on Sarah from the Patek Philippe shop. "The one at Stanford Mall." That was the address the receipt had indicated. "But I don't have the purchase date. It was torn off."

"I'll ask around the stores there," Jim said, taking a wide tape and imprinted my fingerprints on them.

How had the burglar, a total stranger, known I always cracked that window a tiny gap every night? Or, would he have pried it open if it had been closed? The window had been ajar when Sarah and I had checked the place to see how he'd gotten in. My need to keep the air circulating had been a cause of contention between us since the day she moved in, and now I was filled with remorse for my pig-headedness.

Jim jolted me out of my musing. "I'll park on Emerson tonight." He jerked his chin toward the window facing the Street. "Tomorrow morning, my partner—he goes by the name Alias—will take over at six for a couple of hours, till you girls leave for work. When's the alarm getting put in?"

I didn't bother to state I'd be out to work by five, as Sarah would be home till at least nine, and I didn't want her unwatched. I glanced at Sarah's bedside clock. "Sarah's making the arrangements. It's not like her to be late."

I looked out her bedroom window to the Emerson Street below, but there was no sign of her green coupe. Images of Sarah struggling with the burglar as he tried to kidnap her wafted through my head. Perhaps I should have been with her the whole day.

"Your landlord's okay with the alarm?" Jim asked.

"He's ecstatic. Sarah's getting a fancy one, with microphone capacity, so the security company can hear if someone breaks in once the alarm's set."

As if on cue, Sarah stepped into the living room. She must have already parked in the basement when I'd looked out.

"Hey!" She extended her hand at Jim, her face slightly flushed.

Jim handed her his business card, which she glanced at and slipped into the dark green notebook. She'd kept it in her Louis Vuitton backpack. I saw for the first time that she had many other name cards tucked between the pages of the book.

Who were these contacts? Would she notice she'd lost Jackson's? I waited for her to replace the notebook, hoping she wouldn't see that Jackson's card was missing.

❖Chapter Ten❖

AFTER JIM LEFT, Sarah asked, "So, you think he's trustworthy?"

He was to return later for his all-night guard duty.

"I don't think he works for the government." I winked at her, and she rolled her puppy-brown eyes at me.

"The alarm people will get here in thirty minutes," Sarah said. "You don't have to wait. I know you have work."

"Don't I have to learn how to set the alarm, etcetera?"

"They'll run through the details with me. I can explain to you."

This arrangement worried me, since I was mechanically challenged. If I punched in the wrong code or sequence, I might bring the entire police department to our place. Or worse, break the device.

Back at Stay Fit I tidied up the cubicles behind the counter and noticed a cell phone set by one of the member's duffel bags. Sheila Wyatt, a morning regular. I drew a deep breath and picked it up.

Zumba music vibrated throughout the entire floor, a dead giveaway of where I worked for the person on the other end of the line. I mumbled something about the bathroom to Susan Summers, and zipped to the ladies' room.

Huddled in a toilet cubicle, I punched in Jackson's number. It probably wasn't one of my proudest moments, but if Sarah's P.I. had vanished as she'd insinuated and the cops got a hold of Jackson's incoming call list, they'd want to know why I'd contacted him. How else could I have called without having the number traced to me? Besides, it was a local number, and I was just borrowing Sheila's phone, I pacified my conscience.

The call was picked up after the second ring. "Anderson and Partners, Attorneys-at-Law. May I help you?" It was a Southern woman's voice.

Jackson's a lawyer? "I'd like to speak with Mr. Anderson, please."

"May I know who's calling?" her sing-song voice went on.

My heart thumped so loudly I was sure it rivaled the drum beat of the Zumba music now only faintly in the background. "I'd like to hire Mr. Anderson for a case." I heard footsteps as someone entered a stall next to me, and I held my breath. A stall door clicked shut.

"Do you have a name, Hon?" the southern woman insisted.

I tried to buy time by hemming and hawing, for it wouldn't do if whoever was in the cubicle next to mine recognized my voice and overheard me issue a fake name.

When I heard the toilet next door flush, I said, "Is Mr. Anderson in?"

"May I tell him who's calling?"

"I'll call back. Thanks." I clicked the phone off. The other bathroom user was washing her hands, so I waited and flushed the toilet to give myself an excuse for taking so long.

So, Jackson was technically not a P.I. although attorneys have been known to hire P.I.s for their business. If Jackson hadn't been available, the receptionist—at least, I assumed that's who she was— would have said she'd take a message, or something like, "Sorry, can you call back later?"

But, if Jackson was in the office, what did that mean? Was Sarah lying to me? Or, was Jackson back from his mysterious vacation? Should I broach the subject with Sarah? Maybe throw some doubt about hiring Jim, and force her to call Jackson in front of me, so I could verify if she was telling the truth about him?

When the coast was clear, I slipped out of the bathroom and casually returned the borrowed cell. Later, I could do a reverse lookup online on my own phone and locate Jackson's office. Maybe drive there on my way to Starbucks and see for myself.

On my Samsung I Googled "Jackson Attorney" and saw his name listed as "Attorney-at-Law." Maybe he provided protection for his clients, too. However, I couldn't find an address for him. Pages on the sites I'd clicked on, said in fine print, "By referral only."

When I got home after my Starbucks stint, I set off the alarm by mistake, as Sarah had forgotten the sequence to disarm the motion detector.

"It'll take pictures of the person who triggers the system." She pointed to the small cameras above the door and also the one aimed at the balcony. I waved at the camera and flashed my teeth at it. "But we can set a five-minute grace period for us to punch the code." She proceeded to do just that.

I wasn't sure I'd remember the precise de-coding. And a few times when I repeated the sequence I got these wrong.

"You're hopeless!" She shook her head at me. "Let's just use the basic system first. Once you're used to that we'll add the photo capture and voice capacity."

"Well said, Watson." I tried to get her to relax.

"I'm the smarter one," she said. "I should be Sherlock."

"Hah! So, you're okay dishing out two thousand for Jim's four days' work?" It sounded like highway robbery, but Sarah didn't seem perturbed by the hefty payroll. I couldn't even chip in ten bucks on my tight budget, what with car insurance and saving for college which at this point didn't look promising.

"It'll be cheaper than paying for my funeral." She sashayed to her bedroom, her Louis Vuitton backpack hefted over one shoulder, and slammed the door.

She was somewhat uptight that night. If she had a boyfriend I'd have said love issues, but she never mentioned anyone.

"And don't touch the alarm!" Her voice was muffled from inside her bedroom but, I still heard her annoyance.

❖Chapter Eleven❖

LATER THAT EVENING, when my mom called right before I dozed off, I almost told her of the burglar. I caught myself as soon as she complained that Keith hadn't called her for two weeks and that she and Dad couldn't even reach him. My brother was pushing twenty-eight. He had his own apartment, his career, his life to lead. Maybe he was busy with work or a new girlfriend. San Francisco, after all, provided a single male with an active night life, (most of which my parents disapproved of—not that this flustered Keith).

Then there were the restaurants. The City by the Bay boasted the most eateries per square mile of any city in the US. I could see why Keith would keep his distance, with my parents poking their noses in every cranny if you'd let them in.

"I'll let Keith know, if, and that's a big *if*, he contacts me." I hadn't heard from Keith since I'd moved to the apartment. The last we'd met had been at our parents' home, when I'd gone to retrieve my old desk, using Mrs. Mott's U-Haul truck. He'd asked for my address in case he wanted to send out Christmas cards this year, scribbling my details on a slip of paper. I was sure he'd lose the scrap in a jiffy. Why not key into his iPhone? All for appearances' sake, I'd noted to myself.

"How's that new roommate of yours getting on?" I heard Mom stifle another yawn.

"We're getting on."

"Seems like a lonely girl. Does her family call her much?"

How about never? "She only has that one brother, Todd. And they're estranged."

"What a shame. You're a good friend to her. Dad and I can tell."

I suppressed a yawn. It's interesting how when you see or hear someone yawn, you fall under the same spell, as if yawning was contagious. But then again I'd only gotten two hours of sleep the night before.

"Tell Lilly I miss her." I glanced at my bedside clock. Ten-thirty! So late already.

"You can come by and hug her yourself. And Brie, Pastor Perry asked for you last night."

Pastor Perry had been "asking for me" since the day I'd felt church wasn't for me. Church worked for some people—kept them in check or, like my parents, gave them a chance to mingle with others they could try to help out. A social agenda. A safe community of generally polite folks. In ours, Evangelical Church of Grace, someone was always trying to wangle a free service from my dad, since he was a doctor. It's not that he made a ton since he paid his own practitioner's insurance, which was tantamount to half his income. Mom tutored, so she'd gotten popular, too.

"Tell Pastor Perry I'm fine."

Keith and I had never seen the practical benefits of church. I'd never boozed, slept around, or been too left- wing. And Keith? He was not the Casanova type, as far as I knew. My little sister, Lilly, always tagged along everywhere my mom went, so at least Mom had one child left with her who was still in the faith.

"You should tell Pastor Perry yourself." My mother definitely sounded annoyed.

"Maybe." I yawned loudly.

"I'll tell him to call you. How about that?"

"Gotta sleep, Mom."

"Before I forget, someone called you this afternoon. Said he's Sarah's friend."

"You gave him my cell number?"

"We can't go about dishing your number around to strangers. I can't even verify him as *your* friend." Mom was beginning to sound as paranoid as Sarah.

"So, is there a name? A number I can call?"

"I wrote it down." I heard rustling in the background. "A Mr. Anderson," she said. "Jackson Anderson. And here's his contact." And she rattled off a string of numbers. "Do you know him?"

"Oh, him." I tried to sound casual, but my heart beat like a war drum. "Sure, I have his number with me, as a matter of fact."

"Is he a new friend?" *Again, she's all nosey.* "He's not a boyfriend, Mother."

"Let me read you his number again, anyway."

Mother was pedantic that way. That was what happened when you were married to a brain doctor for thirty years, I supposed. Everything had to be precise.

Might as well indulge her. "Okay, shoot."

"It's 650-555-2441."

I scribbled it down and hoped she heard the pen scratching on the notepad.

"Okay, gotta sleep, Mom."

"Be nice to Pastor Perry when he calls."

It was a good thing I'd written it, because when I checked Jackson's calling card later, it was not the same number. Not even close. 650-500-7456, his embossed card said. Maybe he'd graced me with his personal contact. How special.

❖Chapter Twelve❖

I **TOSSED AND TURNED** the entire night, wondering about Jackson and why he'd tried to reach me. He must have found out I'd called him earlier. How? Had Sarah, having reached him, confided in him about the burglary, after all? Why hadn't she mentioned it? Perhaps he'd insisted she inform the cops, hence her moodiness. I glanced at the clock. The green numbers said 12:16.

Finally, tired of arguing with myself, I slumped to the window for some fresh air. Outside on the street below, Jim's light blue Crown Victoria sat. I'd only met him that morning, but something about Jim made me trust him. Funny thing about vibes—it was hard to tell if they were dependable clues.

I decided to call him.

He picked it up on the first ring. "Jim, it's Brie."

"Hey, Cheese Girl." He snickered.

"Ha! Ha! I know Sarah's paying you, which technically means you work for her, but could you keep a secret?"

Silence on his side for two seconds. "Depends.

It's not a plot to oust her, is it?"

"Why would I spoil the amazing deal I have, huh?"

"Okay, shoot."

"Remember, you can't breathe a word to her."

"Kid, I was a cop for twenty years. I know how to keep my gap shut."

"Could you check out someone? He's an attorney. I need to find his office address."

"Practicing in California?"

I gave him Jackson's name and the phone number on the embossed card. With his contacts at the sheriff's office, Jim should be able to help. "Make sure it doesn't get traced back to me, okay?"

He grunted. "All right. I won't ask what this is about. I'll call you later, maybe before noon."

When I laid my head on my pillow, I slipped into a fitful sleep, if it could qualify as sleep. In my dream, or maybe I should say nightmare, Keith visited me with his yellow Corvette. He drove up Emerson, and as I crossed the road he tried to run me over. I bolted up to my apartment, but when I stepped inside a masked intruder bashed me in the face with Sarah's Louise Vuitton backpack, which felt as if it had bricks inside.

I tried to scream but a hand reached out and

gave me my cell phone, and a male voice kept saying, "Call! Call!" sounding almost like a crow cawing.

I awoke with a start and tried to make sense of the jumbled scenes. Rarely did I remember dreams, but this one had been so vivid I pinched my arm three times to convince myself I was actually awake and not trapped in the hellish room with the cawing cell phone man. My heart raced so fast it felt as if I'd sprinted on a treadmill. This was the second time I'd been plagued by a nightmare.

How long could I last before my system collapsed due to sleep deprivation?

Once in junior high, I'd discussed dreaming with Pastor Perry during a Bible study at church. He'd shared his tragic experience. One morning, years back, he'd said, he had called his adult daughter, Sasha, after he'd had a bad dream about her. He'd begged her to stay in her apartment, for that day, but she'd scoffed at him.

That evening, Sasha had met with a fatal accident. A drunken trucker hàd flattened her car while she'd been carefully minding her business on Highway 101. Pastor Perry said he'd cried for days after, wishing he'd insisted Sasha heed his words. Even then as he told me his eyes had turned red.

I asked what significance this had for our Bible study and he'd talked of Pontius Pilate's wife. She had dreamed about Jesus and how Pontius Pilate needed to have nothing to do with Jesus' death, but

Pilate had not listened.

"What happened to Pilate's wife?" I'd asked.

"Church tradition says she became a Christian. At least, according to a second-century historian, Origen. And that possibly her name was Claudia, the Claudia mentioned in the book of Timothy."

I wished I'd asked if the Bible recorded other dreams that warned people. But I was no pastor, or biblical student. Could my dreams ever mean more than just a reaction to acid reflux, or an overactive imagination? Or maybe a paranoid and finicky roommate? If I had some time I could research about dreams. But who had that luxury these days?

I rubbed my eyes and dragged myself to the window. Jim's car was gone. It was already five, and the sky was lightening. If I didn't hustle I'd be late to open Stay Fit for the fitness geeks.

As usual, Sarah slept in, and I never saw her when I left for work. I stayed on edge waiting the whole morning for Jim to call about Jackson, even as I was checking in fitness enthusiasts into the Center.

At about eleven, Jim finally buzzed me. "So, what's the scoop?" I asked.

"Did you run a background check on Sarah's family before you took her in?" He didn't sound friendly.

❖Chapter Thirteen❖

RED FLAGS FLASHED ALL ABOUT me. At eighteen and a half, background checks did not rank high on my list of things to look out for in a roommate.

"So, they killed someone? *Sarah* killed someone?" Oh, mercy! My mother would pull me home by the ears. Or Keith, after volunteering to kidnap me so my parents could lock me in a tower and throw away the keys, probably in Loch Ness, would laugh all the way as he drove back to San Francisco. I can just see him and his drinking buddies joking about me in a downtown bar.

Jim cleared his throat. "Her brother, Todd, has been missing for the last nine months. He left for Europe and never came back. An uncle, their dad's younger half- brother, Stuart McIntyre, filed a missing person's report in California and in West Virginia on Todd, even though Todd's bank account showed he's been actively depleting his monthly trust funds."

I wanted to get the name straight. "Stuart, like in

the spelling Stuart Little?"

He let out a low chuckle. "That's the rodent, all right. Anyway, Stuart accused Sarah of foul play, but the court dropped the case, naturally, and Sarah's attorney, Jackson Anderson, accused Stuart of trying to get her into trouble, since Stuart stood to be a benefactor of the fortune if Todd or Sarah ended up in prison, or dead. So, Sarah, in order to steer clear of Stuart, has been in hiding from her uncle, or so my sources claimed."

That was a lot to process. But it explained Sarah's secrecy. "Is this Stuart in cahoots with Todd?"

"Doesn't seem like it. He must have filed a missing person because, if Todd's dead, he'd stand to gain, too. I get the feeling this Stuart is just keeping his fingers crossed for one of them to hit the grave before he does, which is unlikely. Or commit a crime he can prove."

"So Todd's not Sarah's beneficiary if anything happened to her?"

"That's the strange thing about that will. Todd *could* be the beneficiary if he stayed clean, and outlived Sarah. Stuart only gains if Todd's found stained in the eyes of the law or her grandfather's will in any way. But the unfair part is, if anything happened to Todd, Sarah won't gain a thing—it's Stuart who'd benefit." Jim let out a sigh as though the family saga weighed him down, too.

Sarah must not have realized this. In all her attempts to stay on top of things this detail might have slipped her. But who was I to correct her of this, and besides it wasn't like either Sarah or Todd was at a ripe old age.

"How much would I owe you for all the info? Do you charge like an attorney, by the one-tenth of an hour?" I asked jokingly. Some lawyers billed two hundred every ten minutes—and that's US dollars, not Thai Bhat, mind you. I cupped my palm over my mouthpiece and whispered, "And what about Jackson?"

"Mr. Jackson Anderson's an attorney. He was practicing in West Virginia but came here a few years back."

"A few years back?" So he must have moved here first.

"Four years back, actually.

He's the McIntyre solicitor and has been so the last two decades. Apparently, he's been advising Sarah on her financial matters for years. But, he advises on the entire estate, too, not just Sarah's affairs."

"And he's not missing?"

"Who? The brother, Todd?"

"No, Jackson, the attorney."

"Who gave you that idea?"

"Never mind. Did you actually speak to him? To Jackson?"

"I got Jackson's address and drove by the building on University Avenue in Palo Alto. His name's there in the lobby directory. But, it's high-security, and you need to get a pass from the guard desk to call on Mr. Anderson.

I didn't realize you wanted me to speak with him and I didn't check if he's missing. Did you want me to contact him?"

"No-no, that's all right. How much do I owe you for this work?"

"Consider it a bonus, kid. Pete mentioned you hold two jobs to save for college. I guess it's costly to get to the Big Apple and get an acting degree. Maybe we'll see you on the big screen someday, huh? Heard you won some awards in school for some plays."

Big-mouth Pete, even if he meant well. "Some, but not enough to get a full-ride scholarship." Truth was, as long as I stayed home at my parents', schools would never consider giving me a tuition free status, as they'd look at my parent's income, and I couldn't qualify for a student scholarship based on needs. Colleges forgot I'd become my own person now and need to fend for myself.

That's the thing with turning eighteen, you're tried as an adult if you commit a crime, but in some things the law treated you like a minor and still hitched you with your parents. It also didn't help that my parents didn't approve of acting as a choice career and would never willingly support me. My dad had actually hoped I'd go into medicine as I was always good with chemistry.

"Seriously," I said, "how much did it cost to get all that information?"

"Seriously, consider it a treat, okay?"

I never liked to be beholden to others, even if he was kind and meant to be civic-minded, and especially since I wanted to keep this digging from Sarah.

As if he read my mind, Jim said, "I won't breathe a word to Sarah. Just wanted to be sure you girls stay safe. I didn't see anything strange last night. Maybe it was a common robber trying to get rich quick with that Patek Philippe but had to settle for a Rolex. Although he must have stalked Sarah for a few days. She got that new watch a few days back."

"Appreciate it, Jim."

"One more thing. I put a file together for the info I dug up on Mr. Anderson. I can drop it off at your place later, if you want."

Sarah would want to know if she saw Jim pass me anything, especially since she was footing the bill. "What if you passed it to Peter, instead? We see each other practically every day."

"Sure thing, kiddo."

That was the last I spoke with Jim.

❖ Chapter Fourteen❖

It was hard, concentrating on my ten-dollar-per-hour job that afternoon. Why had Jackson tried to contact me? Was he keeping this from Sarah?

That evening, while Sarah and I wolfed down takeout at the round breakfast table, I braced myself for excuses from her. I had to get it off my chest. "Why'd you lie about Jackson? He's not missing. He called me."

She looked up from the Panda Express box, honey walnut shrimp dangling from the end of her chopsticks, and gaped as if I'd broken some eternal promise. "How could you?" Her puppy-brown eyes seemed larger than normal.

"Could I what? Jackson called my mom. Kindly explain that? How'd he get my parents' number? It's *unlisted*."

"When? When'd Jackson call you?"

"Yesterday. And stop skirting. If we are roommates, we have to trust one another. Why'd you lie?" I hoped she was not a serial liar. Lying could be addictive. Once you start it could be hard to stop.

"I didn't lie." She genuinely sounded hurt. "Jackson went missing for a few days. But he came back. Maybe Martha didn't know where he went or something, but he always told me, and this time, no word, nada." She narrowed her eyes at me until they became slits in her face. "Why'd he call?"

I shrugged. "So, you have no clue why?"

"Maybe he wanted to check you out. Confirm your references. Make sure you're a safe bet. He's protective that way. Since my dad died, he's like a father to me. And he's pissed with Todd."

"And where *is* Todd now?"

She shrugged. "My informants weren't sure this time. The last sighting was two weeks back. Maybe he's off the coast of Majorca? Todd's secretive. The curse of the McIntyre clan. We always have to be suspicious, always cautious, always looking behind our backs."

It didn't sound like something I could live with. But as it turned out, it was something I'd ended up doing, too.

At least her story of Todd corroborated with what Jim had said. "Well, most brothers are very private. Like mine. Keith. I never know what he's up to. Never shares anything. Not even a girlfriend's name. Drives my parents nuts." I picked up a piece of Kung Pao chicken with my chopstick and dropped it into my mouth. "So, Jackson knows about the break-in?"

"He'd chain me to a bodyguard if he found out." She left me specifics on what to say and what to avoid when I spoke with Jackson. "Best call him at ten. That's when he's in a relaxed mood, right after his first round of golf. Less likely to grill you like the Spanish Inquisition."

I chewed on the Kung Pao and considered prodding about her uncle, then changed my mind. She tended to clam up when backed to a wall. I'd noticed that when I'd asked about a boyfriend when she first moved in. I needed her to open up more. It was one thing to keep things private, but trust was a different issue. I couldn't share my space with someone with whom I couldn't relax.

That night, I was plagued by worse dreams: intruders with ski masks, whispers of murderers plotting to do away both me and Sarah. My mind tended to take over when I was stressed. Nights were the worst. Things I couldn't process in the day came crashing down, and re-arranged themselves into illogical plots.

I awoke with sweat clinging to the back of my T- shirt, and when I glanced at my bedside clock, I saw that it was about to buzz. Why bother sleeping with only a sliver of time left? I hadn't even checked if Jim was down on the street before I'd slipped between the covers the night before—I was that tired. So, I hopped off the bed, shoved my feet into my bunny-eared slippers and, almost tripping over the area rug in front of my bed, shuffled to the window. I drew back the curtain and squinted out into Emerson Street.

It was still dark outside. The street lamp, its florescent light a dull gray, flickered, probably due to a bad connection.

Jim's blue Crown Victoria wasn't where it had been parked the first night. In its place stood a dark red truck. Maybe a Ford, from what I could see with the dim street lights. It could have belonged to anyone living in the apartment building—although most residents parked in the unsecured underground car lots. Then I noticed something else. Someone wearing a white terry robe leaned against the driver's side door, speaking with the truck's occupant.

Sarah!

What was she up to? She usually slept in till nine or ten—woes of the rich and, at the time, not-so-famous. I quickly drew the curtains closed and peeked out. I hadn't turned the lights in my bedroom on, and dawn hadn't approached that April morning. Had she seen me? I doubted it. She'd poked her head almost all the way into the cab of the truck. Was this Jim's replacement for the morning shift? Alias? Sarah sure was acting friendly.

She'd leaned all the way in, possibly to kiss the driver. I felt bad spying on her but I was drawn to watch. I wanted to find out more, but the clock was ticking, so I left it at that and took my shower. Maybe this was the secret lover she was jealously guarding from me. I guessed she was honoring our contract of no boyfriends allowed in the apartment. Or maybe she thought I would steal him from her for I always felt she saw me as unable to snag a guy on my own.

By the time I'd showered and poured granola into my bowl Sarah must have returned to sleep, for I heard her soft breathing when I placed my ear to her bedroom door. And, the red truck wasn't there when I drove past the front of the apartment building on my way to Stay Fit. Jim must have thought it was safe for us to be left alone. Or, maybe Sarah didn't like having another person know of our break-in...or spying on her secret boyfriend. Maybe she'd talked the truck driver out of guarding us by being extra-friendly. I didn't exactly require sainthood as a criterion for a roommate, although in hindsight, perhaps I should have.

It was a bustling morning at Stay Fit. Office workers rushed to sneak in an hour's workout before showering and shooting off to work. Pete called in sick, and I had to cover for him. I was surprised that I actually missed having him there at the front desk with me. In some ways we worked well as a team. A good friend would have been nice to have that morning. Later, though, he called my cell.

"Did Jim go by your place last night?" No chit chat, simply straight to the point, which was unlike Pete.

"No. But he might have been parked outside. Why?"

"My nephew, Trevor—that's Jim's son I told you about—called me and said Jim didn't come home this morning to take him to school. I had to drive Trevor, since he'd already missed the school bus."

"Maybe Jim has another job." But, the tiny prickles on my back started to make me feel cold. Jim had found all that information about Jackson and the McIntyre family. Who had he asked? Had he gotten into trouble on my account? *Stop dramatizing, Brie Cheese*, I told myself.

"If Jim calls," Pete said, "tell him to contact me, okay? I feel lousy with this head cold as it is, and I need to rest."

"Sure."

"Oh. There's a brown envelope for you in your cubby. Jim passed it to me last night before I left."

The info on Jackson Anderson. Had something serious happened to Jim? It was too obvious to look through the brown envelop, so I left that for later.

I'd better call Mr. Jackson Anderson and demand some answers. Maybe I should tell my dad, just in case.

And this was where I made a judgment error.

Call it youth's folly, but I didn't want my parents butting in, and besides, I wanted to prove to them, and myself, that I could make it on my own. Make ends meet. Be a full-grown adult.

But, some lessons can only be learned the hard way.

❖ Chapter Fifteen ❖

WHEN I CALLED JACKSON'S cell right after ten, as Sarah had advised earlier, he picked up almost immediately. I'd used my own cell phone this time and had used the number Sarah gave me.

"Jackson," he said. His voice was scratchy, as if he'd smoked too much. And he had a touch of a Tennessee drawl.

"Mr. Anderson? This is Brie O'Mara, returning your call."

"Yes, of course. Glad to hear from you."

After the usual pleasantries he said, "I am concerned about Sarah sharing the apartment with you."

"Why?"

"I don't know how much she's told you, but her uncle is out to get her, and the security, or lack thereof in your place, just doesn't measure up with protocol I am used to for my client."

Protocol? "We put in an alarm system two days ago. And we even have some security." I hoped I didn't sound defensive.

"I didn't see a guard at the entrance."

It's not the Ritz Carlton. "What do you suggest, Mr. Anderson?"

"Maybe you can coax Sarah to move out. I can get her a more secure setup. And, just for good faith, I'll pay her share of the rent till the end of the year. That way, you're covered."

That sounded dandy. But, was I truly "covered," whatever that meant? Jackson must have caught wind of the break-in. I didn't dare to bring it up, just in case he didn't. But who'd told him?

If Sarah vacated the apartment, and the supposed burglar came back, he might mistake me for her. We were almost the same build and height. She could easily pass as my sister, or even me, with her large eyes that mirrored mine, except hers were brown and mine blue. Of course, nobody could tell that when we were asleep. What if the uncle, bent on getting rid of her, mistakenly did me in? Security posts and alarms would not deter Uncle Stu, from what I'd gathered. I considered reporting the break-in and getting the cops involved. I resolved to convince Sarah of this.

"Brianna? You there? " The drawl jolted me.

"Yes, yes. Can you give me a few days to think?"

"Two days. I can't take chances on Sarah's life. She's more than just a client to me. Call me at this number when you're ready." Click. I was left with a hollow echo in the phone.

I texted Peter: "How's Jim?" Was he safe? Was the criminal behind our break-in responsible for Jim keeping low, too? Had he stepped onto something forbidden when he'd gone prying for my sake? Guilt weighed like a sack of flour on my back.

My cell beeped ten minutes later with Pete's reply. "Jim got another job. I have to babysit Trevor, though. Bummer. Might take days off."

"Jim coming by my place later?" I texted him a reply.

"Am I my brother's keeper? LOL! I asked him, too. He'll send someone if Sarah requests."

Peter really cared for me. "His partner? Alias?" I persisted.

"Text him yourself."

Maybe Pete didn't care for me that much. "Kk. Tx."

Still, I was afraid Jim had been hurt, or something as sinister.

I texted Jim again. "Brie here. Coming over, later?"

Two hours passed. Still no reply. Worse, a headache was pinching the top of my forehead, right between my eyes. Peter must have shared his flu with me. Generous of him.

By noon I was a basket case, and I told my manager, Thao Sun, I had to leave. I called Starbucks to get the afternoon off. I grabbed my purse and barely made it home; driving twenty miles per hour and keeping the wheels between the lines was tough. I worried about running over someone and several motorists honked me. Could the cops give me a ticket for driving too slowly?

It was only when I got home that I realized I'd forgotten to take the brown envelope Pete had crammed into my small cubbyhole at Stay Fit. Jim had probably already told me all the important details, but it would have been smart to have kept it in my Mini Cooper. It wouldn't do if one of my co-workers decided to do me a favor and bring it to my place. Or worse, took a peek into it.

However, when I got to my apartment, any semblance of worry I had about the envelope dissipated. I felt so nauseated that any fear I'd harbored about someone waiting for me in the apartment never even crossed my mind. Besides, Sarah was supposed to be home. She didn't have to work to sustain her lifestyle.

I often wondered how she passed her time, and I confess, perhaps with a twinge of envy. There were just so many hours one could waste at the salon. Or the gym. She also belonged to some sports resort that came with massages and complementary beverages. Maybe she was there sipping a margarita, even though she was underage.

"For heaven's sake, I'm turning twenty-one this month," she'd said when I'd approached her on this minor infraction before. "It's not like we're living in the prohibition!"

"Maybe we should be," my mother would have replied. But, I hadn't voiced my opinion to Sarah. Mom would have flipped if she'd known of Sarah's tendency to push things to the boundary. "The law is there to protect you," Mom always said.

"What do you do with all your free time?" I'd once asked Sarah.

"You obviously have not traveled in the realms of books."

"Huh?"

"I could get lost for hours exploring the pyramids in the cool comfort of the library. Better than going to the Sahara and battling mosquitoes and humidity, just to see piles of stones."

"So, you've been to Egypt? Floated down the Nile?" Probably sipping a margarita or two?

"Girlfriend, maybe your question should be, 'where have I *not* been?'"

She professed she usually spent entire mornings and afternoons at the library, her nose lost in a book. Maybe that was where she'd deposited herself this morning: reading her eyes out at the main branch on Holbart Avenue. Or, maybe she was out shopping, her second-favorite time-waster.

I disarmed the alarm and plopped onto the sofa, wishing I had time to waste. To read and travel to distant places sounded enticing. Traveling was something Keith, unlike me, always had the privilege. On second thoughts, maybe I'd waste myself on sleep. At that point it sounded better than globe-trotting. As I lay on the sofa, I couldn't shake away the uneasiness that seemed to stick to me like a second skin these days. Questions attacked my brain.

Should I ask Sarah to leave, as Jackson had requested? What would my mother say when she found out? About me living alone? And Jackson? How come he came over to the Bay Area four years ago without Sarah? He couldn't have cared that much for her to have left her in a West Virginia with a dying father and a sick mom.

I must have dozed off on the sofa; when I awoke it was dark—eight-thirty—and there was no sign of Sarah, or of Jim's parked car, when I peered out the window. Then I realized I'd never turned the alarm back on when I'd entered. At least the sleep refreshed me, and all my senses felt rejuvenated.

I placed my hand on the window sill and breathed in the crisp air. That was probably when I heard it: the *tap-tap* sound coming from Sarah's room. It droned on and on, like an annoying woodpecker drumming on a tree trunk. Atherton had several of those in the more woodsy sections. If there was one thing I loved about living in the neighborhood it was the nature that surrounded our apartment building. Doves cooed in the early mornings, crickets chirped when the sun was setting.

But that evening the thought of nature brought the oak tree outside our kitchen window to mind. Jim was right. Someone could climb the branches and reach our balcony easily. And what if someone *had* while I lay sleeping? I ran to Sarah's bedroom, placed my ear on her door and called softly, "Sarah."

Had someone sneaked past me and gone to Sarah's room? Was Sarah in there? Maybe she hadn't noticed I was zonked out on the sofa and had walked straight past me, mind lost in the latest conspiracy theory.

"Sarah, you in there?" I whispered. What if it wasn't Sarah in there?

Only the tapping answered me, as if cajoling me. What if Sarah had been in there the whole time and was lying on the floor, injured? My imagination took over. I had to find a way to get into her bedroom. First I called her cell, hoping she might answer it. No response.

"Sarah, I'm coming in!" I practically yelled.

But, the solid oak bedroom door was locked. This was like her. She'd never left her bedroom lock unfastened without being asked. Did she think I was going to murder her in her sleep? I jiggled the doorknob. Bashing the door down with my shoulder wasn't something I'd consider.

At five-feet-six, and a hundred and twenty pounds, I was no Rambo.

❖ Chapter Sixteen ❖

I WASN'T ON FRIENDLY TERMS with any of my neighbors—how could I since I was hardly around? And Mrs. Mott was gone. I *could* call Mr. Yamamoto and beg the spare key out of him without scaring him with details, but that could take hours, since he lived in Marin, and if Sarah was hurt, we'd have to explain all sorts of things to Mr. Yamamoto. He might even break my lease— a sobering thought since I'd gotten this apartment at such a bargain.

I texted Jim again. An ex-cop would surely have the tools to break in an interior door. Ten minutes later, I'd chewed off my fingernails to stubs and still had no luck reaching Jim. If Sarah was hurt, she could have bled to death by now.

I thought of Sergeant Twist's business card, but it was a shred of warped paper after its run through the washing machine. If I called 911 and the cops came, it would be embarrassing if they found Sarah just sleeping with her iPod buds stuck in her ears—not to mention Sarah would be furious with me with her no-cop policy. And I didn't even want to think what Mom would say.

I thought of Keith. We'd never been brother-sister close, but he might figure out a way in. After all, civil engineering was his specialty. Something sensible, my dad had commented about Keith's career too many times—meaning my acting ambition was useless. Keith was at San Francisco, (close, but not so close he could just hop down the street and bother me), but he frequented my area when visiting construction clients. I punched in his number on my cell phone.

"Hey, Keith?"

"What's up, Brie?"

"I need some advice."

"I'm in the middle of something. If it only takes a minute...."

"Quick question. You know my housemate?"

"Sarah McIntyre?"

"Oh, so you spoke with Mom?" It was the first time he'd taken interest in my affairs. Maybe there was hope for our relationship, so I'd mistakenly wished.

"Mom called me. Several times, actually." He sounded annoyed.

"What she say about Sarah? Oh, never mind." I'd never confided in Keith. What was I thinking calling him? First off, he'd think I was nuts; then I ran the risk of what I'd said looping back to Mom. It appeared notes were already passed around behind my back. If I told him, I might even have to explain the break-in to make sense of things.

He cleared his throat. "What about Sarah?"

"It's just a silly roommate thingy. Sorry I bothered you." I quickly hung up before Keith asked unwelcome questions.

It would be stupid to call the cops, I told myself. This could just be a false alarm. I strained my ears, and still the thudding, fainter it seemed now, persisted.

I contemplated what to do as I keyed in the security codes near the front door, something I should have done when I'd first gotten home. Sarah hadn't showed me how to work the camera capture feature yet and I didn't know how to turn that on, so, we could forget about getting a photo ID of any intruder should he pass this way. But at least, if I got murdered by whoever was in Sarah's bedroom, the killer would trigger the system when making a quick exit. Sarah's paranoia was contagious.

The alarm had a feature that showed any window or entry left ajar and it had been warmer those April nights, so most evenings we'd left our bedroom windows open a crack. Sarah's window registered as unsecured on the alarm pad and so I bypassed hers as well as my bedroom's, which I was going to scoot out of.

I scurried to my room and peered out at Emerson Street below. Three stories down. I could survive if I fell. I hoped I wouldn't break my legs. That might affect my acting career.

Neither Jim, nor his replacement, "Alias," had turned up. I sucked in the crisp air a few times to calm my breathing and reminded myself that at least the alarm was on if I got attacked in Sarah's room and the perpetrator tried to escape.

The ledge outside my window spanned only six inches, but in school I'd taken ballet, which made me nimble, and gymnastics, which had given me loads of practice on balance. If I could somersault and cartwheel on a beam four inches wide, I could sashay my way along the ledge that wrapped around to Sarah's bedroom. *Stay positive,* I told myself.

Once my Skechers were off, I climbed over the sill with bare feet. The icy cold of the cement ledge surprised me and froze my toes. It sent chills up my Achilles. I didn't even want to consider what would happen if someone from the street spotted me and called the cops. I might end up on the evening news. I saw the headlines: "Girl Caught Breaking into Her Own Apartment Refuses to Press Charges."

Might be my only claim to fame if I didn't make it in the acting world, I thought.

I dug my nails into the shingled exterior wall, trying to get some balance as I edged along the ledge. In some areas, I barely had a fingertip hold and had to poke my fingers into any crevice I could manage. I refused to think of spiders living in the cracks. A snail probably moved faster than I did.

When my hands felt the coolness of the glass on Sarah's window, I pressed my cheek against it and sighed with relief. I squinted into her bedroom.

Except for a nightlight Sarah left perpetually on next to her bed, the room was dark. I couldn't see anyone in there. Only shadows.

But, the thudding persisted. It was louder, now that I listened through the glass pane. I imagined Sarah lying behind the bed, wounded, and tapping with her knuckles to signal for help. I hoped it was just my years of watching horror movies that filled my mind with such tragic images and that my supposition was not remotely close to reality.

I heaved up the lip of the casement and wiggled it open. Good thing the windows here didn't have screens. Sarah and I had discussed installing them, what with the population of insects migrating into our apartment each time we cracked the windows open even an inch.

I didn't know what to expect when my feet landed with a soft thud on her carpeted floor. Could I get prosecuted for entering a crime scene, even if it were in my own apartment? Had I incriminated myself, since I hadn't notified 911 when I first suspected foul play? I hadn't even thought of wearing gloves.

What if I found Sarah dead, or something sinister, and the cops found my prints all over the sill? It sure wouldn't look good for me. I rushed to the bathroom attached to Sarah's room.

Get a towel, and wipe off where my prints might be, I told myself, even though I still heard the thudding. It seemed more like a tap-tap sound, louder now, sharper, and more consistent. Then I saw it: the cause of the *tap- tapping*.

Water was dripping from the sink faucet and hitting the porcelain sink bowl. Rest and fear must have heightened my senses, and I'd heard the drip of the water in the bathroom when I was in the quiet of my kitchen. Fool!

❖ Chapter Seventeen ❖

"Sarah?" I called, just in case she was sleeping in the room. But unless she was in the walk-in closet or under the bed, the room was empty of human presence, save mine. Sarah had installed the drawers neatly back in the dresser, and the yellow polka-dotted bedspread lay smooth over her twin four-poster bed.

An idea popped into my mind.

The top drawer slid open, to my surprise. Unlocked! There was a keyhole, but she must have not thought to lock it, since her bedroom door was already guarding her privacy. I knew it was wrong to attempt what I had in mind, but something within me urged me on. Although it was not something I was proud of doing, it was a necessary evil, I convinced myself. After all, Sarah was keeping secrets from me that could help solve the burglary mystery.

The room was dim, with the sliver of light from the florescent street lamp and the faint nightlight, but still, I dared not turn on the stand-up lamp next to her bed. I rummaged in the dark. My hand slipped inside one of her silky panties—my makeshift glove to prevent incriminating fingerprints. Nothing but silky and lacy underwear in the top drawer. They must all be of the La Perla brand, knowing Sarah. Three hundred dollars for a pair of flimsy thongs—literally shreds of silk, I kid you not.

I was about to search the next drawer when the alarm buzzed and announced that someone had entered the apartment. Was it Sarah? A faint beeping told me someone had successfully disarmed the code. Sarah! She'd catch me in the act. No time to slip out the window. I quickly closed the casement as I'd found it, ran to the small walk- in closet, and crouched behind her long dresses on hangers. Her clothes smelled faintly of an expensive, musky perfume I was unfamiliar with.

Someone unlocked the bedroom door, and the soft padding of stockinged feet on carpet approached me. I confirmed from the gait it was Sarah.

Something rustled—possibly paper bags being tossed. The twin bed creaked. She must have sat on it. The familiar high-pitched ping of her iPhone 5, I presumed, as Sarah punched in a series of numbers. She hadn't programmed in the contact as I'd seen her do on some occasions before.

"Hi!" she said. A moment of silence, and she let out a low laugh, almost husky-like. "I could be persuaded."

Another set of sultry giggles.

I felt bad for listening in on her private life. I hoped she wasn't going to mention anything graphic.

"Okay, okay. Business time—yep. It's planned. Don't worry… He's gone. Taken care of."

Who was she referring to? Todd? Her Uncle Stuart?

"I don't know. Tonight, probably… It's like Chateaux Margaux. You can't rush it… Soon, baby. Soon."

She sighed, that lost-in-love kind of sigh. Who was the boyfriend she'd kept secret? Red truck man? Why the secrecy? She'd always been forthright about her love interests, or so I'd thought: several boyfriends in high school, in that boarding school in the U.K. and even one in West Virginia who'd cried buckets when she'd left for California.

What business was she referring to? Her trust fund? It couldn't possibly be the coal business her family was in. She detested its implications too much and hardly spoke of it.

It sounded like she rummaged in her purse, or her Louis Vuitton backpack, and then her feet padded across the carpet. Then water in the shower splashed into the stall. She must have been preparing for a shower.

Once she stepped into the stall, I could sneak out and lock her bedroom door by pressing the button on the doorknob. She'd never know I'd been here.

But, who had she been talking to?

❖ Chapter Eighteen❖

IF I COULD GET A HOLD of her phone, I could memorize the number and do a reverse search on the Internet. I've had my issue with some of these online people-lookup services as my mother became a victim of identity theft a few months back. It was so easy to find a person's credit card number, and a quick Google on the victim's name would bring up the phone number and billing address, enough for identity thieves to put two and two together. But I figured I had a valid cause to use the service.

Sarah hummed a tune. "Fluer-de-lis." I remembered practicing it on the piano years ago as a kid. The shower stall door clicked shut. I peeped out from the closet. Sarah hadn't shut the bathroom door. Figured. Thank goodness, the stall door was the frosty glass-type; she couldn't see me even if she peered out from it.

I tiptoed out of the closet and glanced at the polka-dotted bedspread, now nicely taut. Where had she tossed her iPhone? An array of glossy paper bags of varying colors and sizes lay next to her pillows. Someone had been busy shopping her heart out. Her purse, a companion to her LV backpack, lay on the dresser. I unzipped the flap on the LV. No iPhone in there. If I could just get my hands on that phone.

But, I'd already pushed luck too far. Sarah zipped through everything, and she could be done with her shower in seconds. I rushed to the door and slipped out to the living room hallway. I hadn't noticed if her door was locked but depressed the button on the doorknob anyway before I pulled it closed behind me.

"Brianna? Is that you?" Sarah called from her bathroom. *That was close.* Had she seen me?

I tripped over to my bedroom, and quickly but quietly shut my room door. If she opened it she'd find me asleep, and she might think she was just imagining noises. My bedroom was terribly chilly. The window was ajar since I had to jump into bed quickly. I slipped between the covers and closed my eyes. Just in the nick, too.

"Brie?" She ambled in without bothering to knock, as was her habit. Her bare footsteps shuffled toward me and halted at the bottom of my bed.

"Hi," I said, slowly "waking" up and squinted at her.

She was wrapped in her white plush towel and was drying her hair with an equally lavish one.

Egyptian cotton, she'd told me when I'd commented about how soft her towels felt.

"You up? How come you're home so early?"

"I'm sick." That much was true.

She sat on the edge of my bed. "I'm not surprised. With your window wide open? You're trying to set up an insectarium in our home?"

"Ha-ha. It was stuffy when I got back."

She fidgeted and sat closer to me. "You smell of Hanae Mori."

"Hannah who?"

"My perfume. They gave you a free sachet at Nordstrom?"

Would Nordstrom hand out free perfume samples to someone dressed like me? Hair in a perpetual ponytail, wisps flying around, and yoga pants that are not even Lulu-Lemon's. I wanted to say this, but instead I asked, "Where've you been?"

"Now, *that* is a long story, and it actually involves you." She winked at me.

"You went shopping and bought me new clothes?" Why did I say that? Maybe it was because some of her snide remarks about my poor taste in fashion. Saggy pants just didn't make the cut for trendsetter Sarah. Most of us don't have thirty-eight thousand, tax-free, to play with each month.

She squinted and wagged a finger. "Close, but not quite. You must have powerful intuitive powers."

I thought about my past dreams and wondered if that could qualify as intuition. Some of my dreams actually came true. That was why my nightmares of the last two days worried me. Was someone trying to kill us? Both of us? Naturally, intuition wasn't why I'd known about the shopping.

"Wait." With that, Sarah skipped out of my room.

I quickly jumped out of bed and waved the air around me in an attempt to disperse the perfume smell that had clung to my pores when I'd hidden in her closet.

What should I tell Sarah? That Jackson wanted her out of the apartment? That I agreed? She was going to feel hurt, rejected. Always, she'd complained friends were only using her, only after her money. They always betrayed her, once they were done with her, she'd said. But, I was just a roommate. Not her "BFF" or anything. With her money, she could stay alone, although I knew she was afraid to.

She sashayed back into my room, her auburn hair wet and limp; four or five of the glossy paper bags she'd earlier dumped on her bed in her grasp. She dipped her hand into one of these and tossed out first an LV backpack identical to hers, which incidentally looked just as spanking new as this one. From another glossy shopping bag, she fished out a black leather jacket that had that heavenly new calf-leather smell and, still, from the blue sack, a shoebox.

She dumped these all onto my bed. I sat up and stared at the offerings. Amidst all our burglar problems, she was thinking of a Brie makeover. Exactly what the doctor ordered.

"It's not my birthday," I blurted. How else could I explain this overly generous gesture?

"Don't be silly. These are not *birthday* presents. They're too beneath me for that. Wait." She waved both hands vigorously as if they felt hot. Clearly, she was excited. "You're gonna love this one." She pulled out a transparent box. It was filled with something dark red, in a clear container with a black net over it. Hair?

"What do you think?" She pulled out the wig and propped it on one hand. It was about shoulder length, with ringlets on the sides.

"Tell me you didn't scalp someone," I said.

"Fun-neee. But, it *is* real hair. The best wigs are made with human hair, you know."

"You don't fancy my hairstyle?" I asked as I twirled my light-brown tresses around my finger—a gesture I'd seen her do to her own coiffure cut. Some had called me mousey on account of my hair color, and definitely when I'd gone to the salon, the hairdressers always bickered at the amount of hair on my head, but I didn't think my hairdo was that bad. I do try to work the knots out every morning before I ponytailed it.

"Your hair is gorgeous. But, it's too light for *you* to be *me*."

Come to think of it, the auburn wig was the exact shade and cut as hers: bobbed, with a straight bank across the front and ringlets on the sides. Did she want a twin? I opened my mouth to protest. I didn't like the plan, even *before* I heard it.

"Sarah, I have many issues, but a split personality isn't one of them. *Why* would I want to be you? I need to be able to at least boil H2O." Needless to say, I was the one who made her coffee whenever we were home together.

"Shh!" She glared at me and glanced at the window. "I need your help."

"Right. Your uncle wants you dead, and your lost brother, whose exact location no one can pinpoint in the past nine months or so, is seeking to criminalize you? So, you want them to mistake me for you, so they can kill *me* instead…." I bit down on my lips the moment I said "kill" and saw her face droop.

Sarah glared at me. "I know it looks pathetic, but you're the only friend I have. I have other…associates. Jackson, Megan, the K twins, but you're the only person I truly trust."

I sighed.

"Please, Brie. Hear me out—this will be good for you. I'm not just thinking about myself."

Her eyes were already moist. "And how did you hear about my uncle?"

"Jackson may have mentioned it," I said.

"Really?" She looked quizzically at me.

"You don't want me to know he's after your wealth?"

She sat up straight and stared at her French-manicured fingernails as if they were not quite the shade she'd asked for. "I s'pose you'd find out. But I'm surprised Jackson took such liberties to tell you about Stu."

"If you don't trust me..."

"It's not that. But anyway, will you help me? Now that you know what I'm up against?"

"Shoot." I couldn't believe I said that.

With her petite frame, I felt like an older sister; for even though she was only a couple of inches shorter, she had frail bones and mine were thicker. I also had wider shoulders, possibly from the hours of gymnastics, ballet, and swimming I'd reveled in. Not that I had time for any of those things anymore.

Sarah rubbed the heels of her palms on her eyes. "If we can carry out this plan, you could be financially stable. Independent. Free to accomplish your dreams. Always have the means to do *whatever* you want, *when* you want. You'd never have to worry about money, or your mom bugging you, or your dad hounding you about speaking to that Pastor Jerry, or becoming a doctor, like him."

"It's Perry, Pastor Perry. PP." Maybe it was worth listening to her proposal. I could always refuse.

"Jackson wants to control me. I need to disappear, the way Todd did. We, you and I, need to make him, *them* all, think I'm dead, or kidnapped, or something, so I can live my life the way I want. And I'll reward you generously for your help."

"*We*? I'm not going to partake in murder. Or kidnapping. I watch—correction, *used* to watch—TV detective shows. I've learnt a lot from *24*, and *CSI*. And *FBI Most Wanted*. These are federal offences you are suggesting. I could be jailed for life. Hello? This tiny apartment is still bigger than a prison cell."

"Ridiculous." She waved her hand at me as if I were a gnat. "Nothing like that."

"And, what about your inheritance? You're adamant your brother, or your uncle, doesn't get your share, and you want yourself dead? Or kidnapped?" I gestured back at her, as she did me.

❖Chapter Nineteen❖

SARAH LAID OUT THE FACTS. She would get the inheritance, due in a few days, even *if* she disappeared and were presumed dead, as long as her body remained unfound, and she hadn't committed any crime. Technically.

The inheritance would sit in the bank, and no one but she, or the person authorized with the series of numbers and security measures, could touch the loot. It was a loophole in the will her Grandfather Lucas had drawn up six decades ago. Jackson had explained. She'd double-checked this with at least one other attorney.

"Wouldn't Jackson suspect something?" Never fool around with lawyers, I'd been told.

"He might, but what could he do?"

On the day Sarah turned twenty-one, in ten days, she said, the inheritance would automatically be deposited into a Swiss bank account and access to the wealth could be via the Internet or in person. But, she thought her uncle or her brother, or both, as they might be working in collusion—and never mind that they hated each other—would try to foil things for her or, worse, get rid of her. Take her out and they'd only have to deal with one another. Maybe Todd had made a pact with Stuart to get the uncle off his own back. Her best bet would be to make them both *think* she was dead on the day of her birthday and have her body disappear.

"We'd make it seem as if it was a kidnapping gone wrong, or that a lunatic had murdered and stowed my body somewhere. Then I'd never have to look behind my shoulders."

"Why can't you just disappear to Timbuktu or something?"

"Because I won't get any peace till they *believe* I'm truly gone. Just think of how one of them must have found me living here." She waved her hand about. "The will has a clause that states even if I were deemed dead, the money stays in the bank and the bank is beholden not to divulge any information to them or to anyone prying for five years. Client privacy privileges. If they believed I was truly dead, they'd be trying to find the killer, or kidnapper, rather than focusing their efforts on trying to locate *me*."

"Why would they look for the killer or the kidnapper? Wouldn't one of them stand to gain if you died?"

"Think, think." She jabbed her finger at her temple a few times. "They'd have to start somewhere if I'm off the radar. To prove that I'm dead they'd need to find the killer. The *killer* would be their focus. It's not for a sense of justice, I can tell you that. They'd have to *prove* that I'm dead first if they couldn't find the body. If there's no body, there's no crime as far as the bank's concerned and my money sits in my account."

I slumped my shoulders. Poor Sarah. My heart bled for her. So rich and yet a pauper when it came to family love. "But what about Jackson? Surely he cares."

"Jackson's first and foremost a lawyer, and he mustn't know of this detail. They could subpoena him. And force him to admit I'd committed this unsavory act and I'd lose everything. Lawyers can lose their licenses if they're discovered aiding and abetting any sort of misdemeanor."

"So, Todd had to wait till he was twenty-one, too? To get *his* inheritance?"

She shook her head. "The will only takes effect when *I* turn that age. So, my big brother's been waiting on the sidelines since our mom passed away. You see, I couldn't even get the inheritance till I turned thirty, if one of my parents were still living."

"So, your grandpa favored you? That's why it had to wait for *your* coming of age? And maybe that's why Todd's jealous of you?"

She shrugged. "I only met Grandpa Lucas a dozen times. Each year, he'd pop over once for my birthday and once for Todd's. Grandpa was in his late seventies then. Who knows why he drew up the will that way? I'm just glad there's a loophole. Maybe he purposely did it. He had a sharp acumen for business, what with the coal empire."

"But, why would you need *my* help? You can hide somewhere till your birthday, *then* disappear. Like how Todd did it."

"Strange you mentioned Todd. I always suspected he had an accomplice. Maybe it's Uncle Stuart. I tried to stay off the radar when I came to stay with you. A nobody, in a nothing-much apartment." She waved at the room. "Except now I'm sure of one thing. If Uncle's after me, he'll find me. The more I think about it the more convinced I am that Stuart was behind the burglary. Makes more sense."

"Yet your uncle's supposed hit man didn't succeed."

"Maybe next time he will. No matter where, Uncle's eyes will seek me. There are agencies that can search out people as long as they live 'above ground.' I'd still need to get out, get food, you know, live life."

I nodded. "Have a love life."

She glared at me again as if I'd uttered a bad word. "You don't get it. With the way the trust fund's set up, I'd have to make physical appearances to sign a paper at the bank each month. In fact, I think that's how Stu traced me. His spies must have spotted me at the Fremont Bank last time I did the paperwork to move funds there."

"Get a disguise."

She narrowed her eyes at me and smiled that coy way she had. "Who told you my plan?"

Plan? That was something I wasn't much good at. She'd used that word "plan" on the phone in her bedroom.

Something in my brain clicked but still I couldn't place my finger on it, couldn't put two and two together. Jackson's proposal to coax her to move out of my apartment swirled in my mind. I could cut my losses and get a new housemate. But the fact was I really liked Sarah, in more ways than one, and I pitied her.

Also, her plan had a sweet ring to it. The idea of being generously rewarded spelled financial independence, living my dreams, getting to acting school, and who knows, once in New York, I could even seek out Drew. He could be attached to some machine, maybe wanting to reach out to me but couldn't.

Sarah went on. "Once the inheritance gets moved to Switzerland, we get the bank to issue a transfer to Antigua. You're going to love the beaches there." Her pitch rose with her excitement. "White sands, crystal- clear waters, refreshingly cool after a bake in the sun. We don't have to stay at any one place." She looked at my pale legs, and I instinctively pulled down my yoga pants to cover my calves. Not everyone had slim, tanned limbs like Sarah's to show off.

But there were too many questions floating in my head, and I really didn't want to break any laws. I needed time to think.

"I don't have a... passport," I said.

"Least of our problems. This is your chance to break away from the family expectations you've always complained about."

"So, what do you need me to do?" I finally said.

"I take it you're in?"

"I need to hear your entire plan first. I'm not a criminal." It must have been the cool waters and the baking in the sun parts that did me in, or maybe my white legs, or maybe Drew. I could Facebook my friends to get his address.

She brought both hands up as if to show her palms were free from the stains of guilt. "Neither am I. I just don't want to end up *really* dead. Or forever having to look over my shoulder to see who has a knife up in the air. You can surely understand. I'm only trying to get what's rightly mine. Live a normal life."

But I still had my reservations. There must be a more conventional way of dealing with her uncle's threats, not that there was anything *normal* about his tactics. "Why don't we go to the cops? Spiel on Stu, and on your brother."

"With what evidence? Stuart's already marred my name with the cops. They suspected that I may have done away with Todd once. Good thing Todd's account is being drawn on every month. At least that's what pacified the cops. He may have vanished, but he's alive, somewhere. Either hiding from Uncle, or maybe they're in cahoots. Who knows?"

"But why would Todd work with Stu? I thought he hated your Uncle's guts?"

"That may be. But perhaps Todd figured if he helped Stu he'd be rid of the old man. You know, get the monkey off his own back? Anyway, I can only take care of my well-being. I can't take the risk. I need to keep my slate clean. You understand?"

She had a point about the evidence. Jim hadn't found any inkling of who might have broken in, and since then, no one had tried to attempt anything on either of us. Granted, it had only been two days. How long would this false peace last before somebody struck us again? I made a mental note to get the brown envelope still lying in my cubicle at Stay Fit.

"So Jim couldn't find anything about the burglary?" I asked. She might have told him to drop the case.

She shrugged.

I persisted. "He never called you?"

"Gave him the money and he split. End of story. So are you going to help me?"

I said, "I'll try my best to help. I can't promise anything, though."

"Cross your heart you won't say a word to anyone?"

I'd already kept the burglary a secret from my family. Jim hardly counted, he was a P.I. and, as a professional, he'd done it for the money. So I crossed my heart and gave her my Scout's honor, even though I'd only done a year of scouting.

She leaned over and gave me a quick hug. "This is going to be so fun, too!" She picked up another glossy paper bag, similar to the one that held the wig, and with a flourish brought out another hairpiece. Mousey brown. My shade of mouse.

She pulled the wig over her crown and tucked her hair under it. "What do you think?" She spun around like a ballerina, and the long hair whipped round as she twirled. She could easily pass as my sister. Or me.

"For the next nine days, we switch identities." She drew two small boxes from another paper bag, this time the smallest of the lot—only about six inches long.

"Eyes." She fluttered her eyelashes.

Inside the boxes were two sets of contacts, one set blue, the other brown.

"But what's the point? There's no way you can take over my jobs. Do you know how to boil water? Let alone make coffee?"

"That's the other thing. You'd need to resign. Like, tomorrow." She tossed the wig back into the glossy bag.

"What? My mother will get to hear about it! She has friends at Stay Fit. Matter of fact, one of them recommended me to the manager there. Mom's going to flip!"

"That's just it. By the time your mother flips, you'll be long gone. And," she wagged her pointer finger at me. "More importantly, independently wealthy."

It occurred to me that maybe Todd had an accomplice which could explain why it was difficult to pin-point his whereabouts.

But was it really Uncle Stu?

❖ Chapter Twenty ❖

THROUGHOUT MOST OF THE NIGHT Sarah explained the plan meticulously.

After I said my good-byes the next day, and of course no one was going to suspect it was my sayonara song, Sarah and I would sign the legal documents, accompanied by Jackson, at Fremont Bank--the one off El Camino Real. All her funds from the trust would be changed to a new recipient: me, Brianna O'Mara. Fremont Bank would take photos of Sarah, as part of the records, when she signed over the transfer to me.

"But...." I protested.

"But, nothing."

"You sure Jackson would agree to this?" Surely, his income would be affected. At least, he'd insist on Sarah having her head checked.

"All you need to know now is that everyone has a price. You find that price and promise you'll deliver. Jackson is a person, like any other."

I wasn't convinced that everyone could be bought. My parents had an encyclopedia full of faults, but I knew some things they'd never sway from, not for a billion bucks. That applied to Pastor Perry too, even though I wasn't exactly drawn to the man. In fact, I hadn't thought much about my ex-pastor until Mom mentioned him wanting to contact me. Maybe I felt guilt but he kept popping into my head.

I opened my mouth to argue this blanket statement Sarah'd made, but she put a finger to her lips and glared at me.

Once the bank checked the propriety of the transaction, which might take a couple of hours due to legality and the need for verification, we would return there in the afternoon, this time with Sarah disguised as me and I as her. This was where my acting skills would come in.

I would adopt Sarah's mannerisms—and this was crucial, since officials there had known her a few weeks. Since no one at the bank knew me, having met me only the morning of the signing, it didn't matter if Sarah behaved like me or not, although I was to act a certain distinct way when I first stepped into the bank—maybe flick my hair or chew on my nails, mannerisms Sarah could replicate easily when she was disguised as Brianna O'Mara.

As the recipient, Brie, who in actuality was Sarah, would be fingerprinted at the bank. Since I'd never gotten officially fingerprinted, Brie O'Mara would forever have Sarah McIntyre's fingerprints.

"But don't the banks already have Sarah

McIntyre's prints on file somewhere? They'd be suspicious if this second set they're taking, supposedly belonging to Brie, matched exactly to those."

"Ah...but the first bank that stored my information took a retina scan for security purposes and this second one isn't as sophisticated. They still rely on fingerprinting."

I never mentioned Jim's having used our fingerprints when checking for evidence during the break-in, since he'd reassured me he'd kept our identities confidential. I'd thought to make sure Jim had destroyed that evidence, but he'd not even replied my texts—taken his pay and split, as Sarah had suggested.

The day after our successful bank operation, we were to dress as each other, pack our bags and scram. Forever after, we had the option to switch identities back and forth, as necessary, but we'd be essentially living as one person—as Brie. Once Sarah turned twenty-one and the inheritance was deposited into her account in Switzerland, Sarah McIntyre could "disappear," even permanently, if she wished. As long as the inheritance account was being drawn on legally and showed activity, even the worst intrusions from her uncle could not stop us from accessing it. That was the beauty of having the funds legally belonging to one Brie O'Mara, who now possessed Sarah's fingerprints. It wasn't as if the bank was going to advertise to Uncle Stu about the changes.

On a day-to-day basis, whether a visit to the dentist or a trip to the Bahamas, Sarah might appear as Ms. O'Mara, mousey-haired, blue-eyed, a little taller, and ten pounds heavier—unless I lost weight, which was something I looked forward to.

"But what about in the distant future?" I persisted. I was going to miss my family's dog, Holly. I wouldn't even be able to say good-bye to her. I used to walk Holly when I lived at home, but Lilly had taken over, now that she'd turned eleven and was only too glad to be the "big" girl, since I'd left home. I'd miss Lilly, too. Would she miss me? But she was busy with school and ballet and her church friends. I hadn't been able to get her to come over for sleepovers since I moved in here.

"How long do I have to avoid contact with my family?" I asked.

Sarah raised her eyebrows and looked at me as if I were insane even to think this an issue.

"And dental records. How about that?" I persisted. "Would they catch us and accuse us of fraud if the authorities can prove we've schemed this switch? Haven't you watched *Law and Order?* They can trace us with our teeth."

She flashed a toothy grin, as if she were in a toothpaste commercial. "You should use your imagination to write a book, or something. You're assuming they *can* get a hold of our jaws to run dental checks. No one's going to stop you on a beach in the Bahamas and have the right to inspect your mouth. Hello? You watch too much TV." She shook her head, and flicked her fingers at me as if I were a mosquito.

I charged on. "What if we wanted to live separate lives? Get married? Would we *always* have to live under the same roof? As the same person?"

I thought about Drew coping with his condition somewhere in New York, possibly even in Manhattan. Would I really never see him again? Would the cost of wealth mean I'd have to give up my dreams of becoming a famous actress? Would I have to give up my future like I'd have to give up my past?

"Nothing is forever." Sarah blew at her bangs.

I studied her movements and told myself to remember that habit of hers.

She leaned toward me, her eyes large and round. "Let's just see how things work the next few months. In any case, it's a small price to pay to get access to all my wealth, won't you agree?"

"So, one day, I could return to being me. Simple Brie O'Mara?"

"What would it matter if you were named Brie or Sarah? Like anything in life, all actions have consequences. If you decide to live in wealth, you'd have to give up some of the luxuries of freedom. All celebrities understand this.

Besides, I thought you'd be glad to get that

acting degree in New York. You can easily get into a Big Apple college with my high school records."

It wasn't like my GPA was that bad. "But what if we got caught?"

"We won't. My sources can give us fake IDs so we can leave the US, and even my uncle with his government contacts, can't trace us."

"So, why don't *you* just live on a fake ID forever?"

"I don't want to be a fugitive *forever*. Besides, it would screw up my access to the funds."

"Have you Googled yourself? How easy it is to find out anything about anyone? Someone's bound to find out our scheme."

"That's why I don't Facebook. I don't even use Google. Don't trust the Russians. They can trace your IP address and find what you're up to. Your IP address is practically a fingerprint. Your DNA. They collect data on everyone. Knowledge is power. I always use the library to research anything and pay cash whenever possible. Untraceable."

"I noticed." I recalled the brown paper bag of twenty-four hundred-dollar bills she'd passed me for her rental deposit. Maybe she'd even paid cash for that Patek Philippe watch; I still couldn't determine what she'd done with it--maybe stored it deep inside that refrigerated safe she had.

She was on a roll. "Think. After we tire of Antigua and the five hundred islands in the sun, we could travel the world, maybe even take up acting in Paris together. They're into all sorts of *nuevo* stage techniques there. Experimental stuff. Why limit yourself to New York?"

She had a point. Of course, I'd never really toyed with the idea of never seeing my family and close friends again, even if I didn't have too many of those. If I vanished, someone would miss me. How long would they mourn my disappearance? How would Dad take it, with his weak heart and all? And how would Lilly fare? But she was young and popular. She'd probably forget me in a jiffy.

I might even see my face on those milk cartons that feature missing kids. But, those pictures were so small; who'd even recognize me if they saw my photo and met me in person? I could afford plastic surgery, get rid of that slight hump on the bridge of my nose, pout my lips like Angelina Jolie. Possibilities. So, I nodded.

"What do you think of the plan?" Sarah's brown eyes widened and sparkled.

Plan. That word again. "Sounds viable." Yet, I still had many questions.

Sarah gave a small shriek and leapt off my bed, clapping her fingertips with glee like a small child just offered a bag of Jelly Bellies. "I knew you'd make a great friend the moment I met you!" She hugged me tight.

We stashed the newly bought items—and there were a few more outfits in there, too—in my closet and cut the paper bags into tiny pieces before stuffing them into the recycling bin. Recycling would come the next day. Convenient.

The evidence would be history by the time anyone tried to piece the jigsaw together or had any inkling of what we were up to. We had two days to pack. Gather just essentials: minimal clothes—we'd splurge on a new wardrobe suited to whatever climate we'd decide on later; favorite mementos we couldn't live without; my laptop, her laptop—at least for now. But she warned that once airborne we'd have to ditch the computers. Nothing must be traceable to us or our whereabouts.

The rest, like our furniture and Sarah's bulky safe, we'd donate to Salvation Army. Our contribution to the less fortunate, she'd said. Sarah had called the Salvation Army in Atherton that afternoon and spoken to the manager directly—I would mail the house key to our landlord with a check to complete the rest of the year's rent.

❖Chapter Twenty-One❖

SARAH RUSHED TO HER room and came back with $18,000 in crisp one-hundred-dollar bills. I would deposit these into my BOA account the next day to cover my check to my landlord. Mr. Yamamoto would be ecstatic, since I'd release his obligations to hold the place, and he'd be free to rent out the apartment and up his investment, since he'd collect double rents.

I did worry about what the FBI or the cops would think, since my bank account would balloon so suddenly. Would the authorities think I was responsible for Sarah's disappearance? What if they put out an APB on *me*? But, I would be out of the country and lying low in another part of the world, Sarah reassured me.

"Shush!" Sarah said. "Such a grandma." And she stooped and hunched her back, and stomped around like Quasimodo.

I laughed so hard I had hiccups, and, shoved my concerns out of my head.

Sarah had detailed our entire errand list for

tomorrow on a yellow writing pad, and we ticked each task off once it was done. She seemed to have thought through everything.

"Nothing must be left to chance," she said.

"So, how long have you been planning this?" I asked while dumping some of my clothes into black garbage bags for the donations. They were mostly non-Lulu Lemon fitted jackets and skinny jeans.

"Since the break-in. Two whole days of planning at the library." She tapped her temple with her index finger.

With the apartment empty, even the cops might just assume I'd just moved on. They might not even classify me as a missing person until a few days had passed. Young adults sometimes wanted to assert their independence, needed their own space. My parents would always have the hope of seeing me again someday. That would keep them going, I reassured myself, but my heart sank at the grief I would initially put them through. With my work resignations, the cops might even pacify Mother with the notion that I needed a change--something I certainly felt I did too often. How long could a person survive on less than five hours of sleep each night?

"Remember," Sarah said before she skipped to her bedroom. It was already past one in the morning; I'd never seen her so energized. "Not a word to anyone. Not even Jackson."

Should I warn Sarah about Jackson's push to

have her leave my apartment? But, if Sarah reneged on her deal and left, I stood to lose. I'd already imagined myself sitting on the beach in the Caribbean somewhere, sipping piña colada with a tiny pink umbrella perched on the rim of the fluted goblet. Nobody would even ask if I were underaged there.

And then there was Drew. My unfinished business. Once things quieted down, I could hire a P.I. to locate him.

❖Chapter Twenty-Two❖

THAT NIGHT, MY NIGHTMARES plagued me even worse than before. Three nights in a row, now. The stress was burrowing into my marrow hence the restless sleep, I consoled myself. In that dream, I witnessed the burglar's return, and this time he murdered me with a knife in my sleep; he stabbed me continuously in my heart, right before Sarah and I could carry out our scheme. I watched my own slaughter. It almost felt like an out of body experience.

When I awoke with a jolt, sweat beading behind my neck, I jotted down the particulars of the dream in a notebook I'd placed next to my bed. The more I dwelled upon it, the more I realized it was similar to the first and second nightmares I'd had, except in those two the burglar had killed Sarah, too. Should I warn her?

Paranoia must be contagious.

What theories would Pastor Perry have about these troubled images in my head? Would he still insist they were warnings, like Pontius Pilate's wife's dream about Jesus? Or, were these just the rambling ravings of a mind on the verge of cracking? The outcome of deceit, a psychologist might conclude. Or sheer fatigue.

But, Sarah was right. It was too dangerous for her to stay in the apartment. Even for her to remain in the San Francisco Bay Area was a bad idea. The scheme she'd concocted would ensure her some safety. It wasn't perfect, but it would buy her time to escape, disappear, provided her uncle or brother didn't discover it before the inheritance came through and we'd managed to run away undetected for a while. Yet, what if Jackson forced Sarah to leave me? I would lose it all. I hoped Jim would contact me tomorrow.

In my soul, I felt I should tell someone of our plan. What if I had to bear the full blame if we got caught? There must have been a law against switching identities, or fooling banks. Unfortunately, I had neither the time nor the energy to Google anything about it.

During our earlier discussion, I'd related my fears to Sarah. "What is this I'm committing? Identity theft?"

"If I gave you permission to be me, how is it a theft? How are you breaking any laws? It's my money. I can choose who I want to bequeath it to." Again, she rolled her eyes and shook her head at me.

I supposed she was correct. But, if she were

accused of fraud, would she defend me and mention it had been her idea in the first place? Would that make a difference? But, of course, I was being paranoid. Why on earth would Sarah, who was so averse to divulging anything to the authorities, want to report me?

.

❖Chapter Twenty-Three❖

THE DIGITAL CLOCK showed 4:16 a.m., almost time to get up, and once again, I'd hardly slept. The lack of rest had turned my brain to Jell-O. It was a good thing this would be the last of my break-of-dawn stints at Stay Fit. I must be the most unfit person that walked through Stay Fit's doors. At the rate I was going without sleep, I doubted my mind could function at full capacity, even if caffeine was intravenously injected into me. I couldn't say I didn't welcome the idea of sleeping in, being a natural night owl.

I scripted out my excuse to Thao, my office manager, about resigning. She was going to be pissed, even if I offered to stay till the end of the day. If Peter wasn't there, I might never get a chance to say good-bye to him—a pity, since I considered him a good friend. And once I left without so much as a farewell, he'd probably never want to speak to me again.

Before I left for work, my cell phone buzzed. Who would call me at five a.m.? I didn't recognize the number, but with all that was happening, I picked up the call. It could be Jim reaching me from his home phone.

"Brianna?" The voice sounded vaguely familiar, but I couldn't put a face to it.

"Yes?"

"It's Pastor Perry." His voice sounded hoarse, like sand paper. Trust him to call at an unearthly hour. "Yes?"

"I'm sorry to wake you up so early, but something terrible has happened, and your mother wanted me to reach you, since she couldn't use her phone in the ICU."

"ICU? What…?"

"It's your dad."

My heart froze. It practically stopped altogether.

"What about my dad?"

"He's had a heart attack."

I sucked in my breath. My worst fears. "How's he now?" My throat constricted, and my mouth felt dry.

"The doctors think he also suffered a stroke, but they can only confirm that later. They believe he has some pressure building in his brain. I will only know the details as—"

"Is he conscious? Is he? " My mind couldn't accept the words spoken to me but my hand grabbed my yellow duffel off the leather sofa and made for the door.

Then, it hit me: how would this affect my plan with Sarah? Her bedroom door was still closed. She was probably still asleep. We'd talked about details till late. Should I tell her everything was off? *What was I thinking when I agreed?*

Pastor Perry said, "I'm afraid your dad's in a coma. He's rambling, sometimes."

"Where is he?"

"Palo Alto Medical."

That was where he worked half the time when he was not in his own clinic. "So, he wouldn't recognize me if I were there?"

"I'm afraid not. But, your mother would appreciate your coming. Lilly's home, with Lupe. Your mother didn't want Lilly to worry, but she could do with your company. We couldn't reach Keith."

I nodded, as if Pastor Perry could see me.

"Brianna? You there?" he asked.

"Yes, yes."

"I can come over and pick you up."

"No. I'll drive over."

"Maybe Mrs. Michaels and I can visit you in that new apartment one of these days."

"Sure." What else could I say? His wife, Jane, was a decent person. Besides, I'd be gone in a few days— *if* I could muster the courage to leave, despite Dad's condition. "Give me an hour," I said, and hung up before he could protest.

I'd never prayed before, not like this, but I wanted to see Daddy before I disappeared. I said a quick plea, as if God were my friend: "God, if you're out there, keep my father alive." Would Dad last long enough for me to see him—maybe for the last time? That Lilly was still home was a good indication that Mom thought he'd hang in there. Otherwise, she would've insisted Lilly went with her. Mom was that way.

This turn of events meant I now had a good reason to give Thao my resignation. Dad was ill, and I needed to be flexible, so better to resign, I'd say.

Perfect. I'd use it on Starbucks, too. I half-hoped Pete wouldn't be at Stay Fit. It was hard to lie to a nice person, especially to someone who might like me too much. Sarah had insisted she'd dropped off her payment to Jim because I had wondered if he was upset with us for not paying, hence the cold-shoulder. I wished I could have thanked him personally, especially since I'd never heard back from him.

"Hey?" Sarah opened her door, rubbing her eyes. "Who were you talking to?"

"Just the pastor I told you about."

"Gawd! He doesn't believe in sleeping in?"

I shrugged. It was unlike her to get up at this hour, and I didn't think I'd been that loud on the phone. But, maybe I had been. Or maybe she was as wound up about our scheme as I was. "He's been wanting to see me."

"You didn't tell him anything, did you?"

"I don't even like him." She sure was suspicious. "I need to work for a couple of hours after I send in my resignation. Don't want them to wonder why I was in a hurry to leave."

"Don't forget the bank, at eleven. You need to be back here at ten, latest. We have a lot to do."

I slung my yellow tote over my shoulder. "Don't forget to put the alarm on." Especially after that nightmare I had, I thought, but I didn't say that to her. I pulled the front door shut before she could bug me further. There was so much to process.

❖Chapter Twenty-Four❖

IT WAS AMAZING HOW MUCH I'd accomplished since my day had started at the break of dawn. I toyed with what I should do about Dad. I hadn't told Sarah, as it would rattle her. She had a knack for making things seem more complicated than they were. If I visited the hospital, Mom might keep me there indefinitely. But I couldn't leave without seeing Dad at least once, especially in his condition. What if he never recovered and I never saw him alive again? Suddenly, I hoped heaven was real.

Don't panic.

I had every intention of returning to some semblance of my old life once Sarah was assured of her inheritance and I'd had my few years of financial freedom and made a stable income, hopefully on Broadway. Or Hollywood. Although I couldn't help but ask myself if there was a price for deception.

It was a full morning at Stay Fit, what with Pete still on sick leave. In the end, I called Mom at eight.

"You coming?" she said. I could tell by the nasalness in her voice she'd been crying.

"I can't just take off." True.

"But, this is a family emergency, for God's sake, Brianna Zoe." I hated it when she used my middle name. Zoe means "full life," like when Jesus preached, "I have come to give you life (zoe) and life more abundantly (zoe)." I doubted my present full plate—as in ultra- busy—was the kind of full life that Jesus meant. I hoped not.

"I'll try later," I said. Perhaps I could dash by the hospital after the bank deal and before my Starbucks resignation.

"Keith's arriving in an hour. Grandma's coming soon. I'm alone with Lilly now. You want to speak with her?"

So, Lilly was there after all. *Dad's condition must have gotten worse.* "I'll talk to her when I get there."

Mom let out a long sigh, which was something I was *not* going to miss. I felt bad enough as it was. Not to mention worried.

Thao accepted my resignation with her thin upper lip in a grimace. She seemed to have more on her mind than my news. In her clipped Vietnamese accent, she said, "As you wish, Brianna."

Everyone was hounded by troubles. That was life.

Take Peter, for instance. He was obviously too sick even to answer my text messages. I thought about which friend or associate I could call or text to say farewell in my last few hours as the "uncomplicated Brie," the not- wealthy but still-honest Brie with the simple life.

After today, Sarah and I would have to restrict our contact with everyone. But, besides my immediate family, I'd lost touch with most of the kids I'd hung around with at church, in high school, and even those from the private ballet academy I used to frequent.

Everyone who was worth hanging out with had accepted huge loans from their parents, the bank, or both, and moved on to college, having started a new phase in life. Except me. I'd toyed with the idea of getting a student loan with the low government interest rates.

But at the end of the day, debt is debt, and I didn't want to start a career with a noose around my neck. That was why this windfall from Sarah could right my path. Make up for lost opportunities. Prove that I could make my dreams come true without help, without intervention from well-meaning parents.

Maybe I could confide in Jackson about Sarah's plan. He was, after all, on her side. Besides legal implications, why wouldn't she want Jackson to know? We could use him as a hedge, in case things went wrong. But, could I trust him not to use the information I confided against me?

Not pursuing my gut feeling and not researching more about Jackson was one of the many slip-ups I made.

❖Chapter Twenty-Five❖

FROM MY JEANS pocket, I worked out Jackson's card—the one I'd snatched from Sarah's dresser and now was crumpled—and stared at it before punching in the digits after his name, instead of redialing the number from the call I'd made to him yesterday. Maybe subconsciously I wanted to see if I could connect with him at this office number, too, after the failed attempt in the toilet stall using Sheila Wyatt's cell.

"Anderson and Partners, Attorneys-at-Law. May I help you?" It was the same Southern woman's voice. Probably Martha, the secretary Sarah had mentioned.

"I'd like to speak with Mr. Jackson Anderson, please."

"May I know who's calling?"

What if Jackson had given me his private line for a reason? Maybe he didn't want anyone, not even Southern-belle Martha, to know he'd contacted me. Would I get into trouble if I left my name?

"Can I just speak with him?" Of course, they'd

have my cell phone number now, what with caller ID.

"Hon, this is a law-yer's office." Martha's drawl conjured pictures of Scarlett O'Hara dressed in her voluminous ball gowns as in *Gone with the Wind*. "If you want ta speak ta a law-yer, you'd need ta at least share your name." She sounded impatient, despite the drawl.

I hung up the phone. *What an idiot*. I should have just called the number that was already in my recent call menu. Before I could press the speed dial, a call came through. I somewhat recognized the number

"Yes?"

"Brianna? This is Pastor Perry, again." No wonder the number was familiar.

"I can't talk right now. I'm at work."

"Your mother told me to get you. I'm outside Stay Fit this very moment."

"Shucks! I mean, never mind. I'll be out. Wait out there." If he came in and found out I'd quit, that would complicate matters.

I grabbed my yellow duffel and breezed out the door.

"Hey!" Thao hailed me as I bolted to the main entrance. "That's it? You not coming back, and no good- bye hugs, even?" Her Vietnamese accent was more pronounced than usual. Stress could even affect speech. I rushed to my cubby hole, snatched the brown envelope from Jim, stuffed it into my duffel, and almost bowled Thao down with my bear hug.

"I'll call you," I hollered, rushing out the door. Someday. One day.

Pastor Perry stood by his white, one-ton Dodge van. It could carry twelve passengers. When I'd asked why he needed something that big, seeing as there were only him and Mrs. Michaels since Sasha's accident two years earlier, he'd said he used it to sleep in when he made cross country trips.

I waved to him and headed toward my Mini Cooper parked five cars down the street. "I'll see you at the hospital," I hollered.

"I'll drive you there and back." He pointed toward the van's passenger side. Its door was already open. "You look too tired to be driving, anyway."

I shrugged. He could be so persistent. No way could I get out of this one. Better be agreeable. I quickened my steps and strode toward him. "How's Dad?" I swung myself into the passenger cab of the Dodge as he revved the engine. "He's a fighter. Keep praying."

I felt guilty. I'd only whimpered out that poor excuse of a prayer. What good would praying do, anyway? When it was time to go, it was time to go, right? That was what I'd heard from Christians and non-Christians alike. Maybe Pastor Perry was a mind reader.

He said, "Prayer works, you know. I have so many stories, I should write a book on miracles. But, enough of me. How's life? Gotten used to not staying home? Must be different staying by yourself, with a new roommate."

He was chatty today.

"Life's pretty good." After all, I was about to have an heiress share her identity, and inheritance with me. And I might even find out about Drew. "Until now. I'm worried about Dad."

"God has a reason for all things."

Like delaying me from becoming sweetly wealthy?

I stared out the window and thought I saw Keith's yellow Corvette rounding a corner. "Is Keith at the hospital?" I twisted my shoulder and craned to look at the speeding car.

"Said he was on his way."

"Did you see that Corvette?" That must have been Keith. The license plate was "2BO..." I didn't catch the rest of it. Keith's' license, "2BOR02B," stood for "To be or not to be." A true Shakespeare fan.

The car must have been his, unless there was another banana-colored Corvette with the same first three letters on the plate. Except, if it was him, why was he heading toward my place? To pick me up?

Suddenly, knots formed in my stomach. If Keith met Sarah and saw the state of my apartment, he would suspect something. My suitcase was in the living room, bursting with things I planned to take with me.

Black garbage bags of our stuff stood piled in the corner of the kitchen. The thrift store was to pick up the day after tomorrow, and Sarah's twin friends, the K brothers, were to take the donations down to curbside for them, so as to avoid suspicions, in case someone I knew popped by and saw our furniture downstairs before we left. Sarah had explained to the twins we were going for an extended vacation. They were oblivious about our upcoming switch.

"Hey!" Pastor Perry's voice jerked me back. "I said I didn't notice any Corvettes. A nickel for your thoughts?"

"Might not be worth that much. My thoughts, that is." I let out a chuckle, which sounded more like a snort.

"I know you don't believe in the things I believe in, but we should chat sometimes. You might be surprised at how much we could actually agree on."

What would he say about me skipping town? I doubted he'd agree with my plans. "We can get together someday, next time."

❖ Chapter Twenty-Six ❖

DAD'S CASE MUST HAVE been worse than Pastor Perry had let on, as my mother was in tears. Grandma Linelle, my Dad's mother, was slouched there on the white plastic molded chair. She looked exhausted. Her white hair poofed at the sides, which was unlike her usual coiffed self. My grandpa, Grandma Linelle's husband of over fifty years, had died when I was three.

"There you are!" Mom rushed to me. She almost collapsed when I hugged her. She was at least five inches shorter than me, so I felt like the parent consoling a younger child. I'd inherited my height from my six-footer dad.

"He's still unconscious, Brie," Mom said. The skin under her eyes looked papery thin with faint blue lines.

"Can I see him?"

"Doctor Chen says only for a few minutes, and only one family visitor at a time. He's so fragile." She broke into a sob.

My sister, sitting next to Grandma, briefly

glanced at me, and looked down at her Mary Jane shoes, which she *tap-tapped* on the linoleum floor. I wanted to hug Lilly and cry together with her, but I couldn't bring myself to look her in the eye. It was better I pulled away from her now, I lied to myself. She was young. The more distance she felt from me, the more she'd realize she could live through problems without me, and the better for her when she awoke one morning, soon, and found her sister had left without a trace. Not even decent enough to give her a proper good-bye. It's only for a season, I consoled myself, as if that made me feel better. I smiled at her.

But inside, I felt like a scumbag.

"Hi, Lilly!" I said when I walked past her and gave Grandma a peck on the cheek. My grandmother looked fragile, too. What had happened to everyone?

"Holly misses you," Lilly said, her eyelids heavy with fatigue.

I flashed my teeth at her again. "Give her two extra hugs and a pat from me."

She nodded.

Nothing prepared me to see my "Doctor Dad," as I'd jokingly called him so many times in my past. Dad's hospital room was dark and smelled of Pine-Sol, the kind of clean scent that dug its way deep into your nostrils and smarted your eyes. The only light came from the blinking red and blue bulbs on a dashboard, some kind of a monitor with wires coming out of it, like an electronic octopus with a rectangular head. Some of the tubes and wires were attached to my dad's arms and nostrils.

Except for the machines bleeping and a soft whooshing that came from another contraption attached to Dad's chest, the room was quiet. Peaceful, even—that is, if one couldn't hear the thumping of my heart rebelling against the sight before me.

When had time and age stolen my strong dad from me? Replaced him with this frail imposter? Where was the father who'd borne me on his shoulders as we'd struggled up the steep streets of San Francisco's China Town, watching turtles swim in Chinese restaurant displays, wondering how we could save them from certain death?

I squinted and blinked rapidly a few times to control my emotions. A nurse stood in a corner, reading a chart. She was very still, like the sentry guarding the Buckingham Palace I'd seen on television.

"You want five minutes with your father?" She spoke with an English accent. Before I could nod, she walked toward the door, eyes still on the chart.

"How is he?"

"His cardiologist will explain later. They're still running tests."

When I heard the door close with a wheeze from the hydraulic pump, I slid to my knees next to my father.

When had he become so small? My doctor daddy. My strong daddy.

"Dad?" I whispered.

His eyelids didn't even flutter. Nothing.

I ran my finger up his hairy arm, the one without the IVs and without needles or tubes attached. Could he hear me? Surely they'd have told me if he was brain-dead or something. People got better from strokes all the time. I knew a mother of five who'd suffered a stroke and had recovered within six months, even though she'd been unable to walk or speak for a couple of weeks after it hit her.

"Dad?" I waited, then stood and kissed him on the forehead. His skin felt cool, too cool. How long would he remain in that state? "It's Brie."

I'd heard those stories of people insisting that you talked to comatose patients. That just because the patients seemed unconscious that didn't mean they couldn't hear every word, even if they showed no signs of acknowledgements. I now understood why people would believe or wanted to believe that. They didn't have a choice. The alternative was almost unthinkable. To see your loved one lying there, and yet unreachable, left you with an emptiness, a loneliness as though someone had gouged your heart out.

"Dad?" I whispered into his ear. "I'll always love you. No matter what. I'll always remember you. Don't forget that. I'll come back. I need to do this. To prove to myself. Please understand."

I heard a grunt, but it might have been just my imagination. Or my own sob. His eyes remained closed. Not even a flutter. I leaned forward and planted my lips on his cool forehead.

Better leave before I changed my mind about the switch. I turned, practically tripped out the door, and rushed to the bathroom before my mother could stop me. If nothing else, she'd understand my need to process this alone.

Later, as I strode back out to the waiting room, Keith, with his designer navy blazer, swaggered in from the entry with that lazy, lanky strut of his. He headed straight toward our mother, his arms outstretched, and gave her a long hug. Our eyes locked for a moment over Mother's head. Had Keith just arrived? It must have been a good thirty minutes when that banana-colored Corvette had whizzed down my road. But then again, we do live in the Bay Area. where corvettes and Teslas abound.

"Just got here?" I asked casually. "Yep."

"How are you holding up?" Keith shrugged.

"He'll get over the stroke. I know he will. He's strong and sixty-two isn't old." A fact I'd chanted to myself over and over in the bathroom.

"I suppose. Still a shocker, though. He was always exercising."

I nodded. "I thought you'd be here sooner."

"Why'd you think that?" he asked.

Pastor Perry pulled Mom away, and they spoke

in low tones.

I looked Keith straight in the eye. "Pastor Perry said he called you earlier and that you were rushing down."

"You accusing me of *not* rushing here quick enough? Some of us have a real job. I can't just up and leave. I had a client meeting."

I supposed waking up at the crack of dawn to dash to work didn't count as a real job in Keith's vocabulary. "I could have sworn I saw your car race past Birch and turn onto Holbart." That was the street that led to Emerson where my apartment building stood.

"I'm surprised you never see me whizz pass your place more often, then. I have clients in the area. I would have picked you up, but you weren't home."

What did he mean by that? "You went by my place to pick me up?" How brotherly.

"I did, but your car wasn't in its usual spot underground, so I figured you'd left. But, I don't know *if* it was me you saw. Like I said, I just got here." With that, Keith stalked off toward Pastor Perry and Mom. Of course, he didn't even realize I'd be at work by eight. It would have been unlike him to think of me. Family tragedies have been known to melt the most hardened of hearts, so maybe there was hope for him.

"Mom, I have to scoot." I broke up Mom's deep discussion with Keith and Pastor Perry. "Let me know about Dad's progress. If you can't get a hold of me, text me when you learn more."

I'd have to talk Sarah into allowing me to keep my cell active a few days more, although she'd talked about us going dark and just making do with twenty-dollar throwaways when we got out of the United States in case the cops decided to trace us via our mobile phones.

Supposedly, these devices could act as GPS beacons. "Traceable," was the word Sarah had used when she'd explained. It'd be harder to trace the twenty-dollar ones, she'd said.

Mom gave me a bewildered stare. "I don't text."

Pastor Perry laid his hand on her arm. "That's okay. *I'll* text Brie, if you want. And, Brie, you be sure to call me anytime you want to talk."

I spun around to run out of the waiting room, sure I would give up on my plans with Sarah if I stood there a second longer.

"Brie!" It was Lilly. She held her arm out, and at first I thought she wanted me to pull her off her seat as I breezed by, but then I saw she was passing me something. "It's for you." She handed me a square envelope.

"Don't open till it's your birthday," she said quietly. My birthday wasn't for another two months. Thoughtful of her. I turned it over and saw it was sealed. It must have been a card.

"Thanks, Sweetie."

"No peeking." She smiled at me. "Promise?"

I nodded. I was going to miss all eleven years of her. I bent down and drew her blonde head into my chest. Maybe one day she'd forgive me, and when I returned I intended to make it up to her. I'd tell her this lousy sister of hers had missed her every step of the way, even as she'd been sipping piña coladas on a beach in Antigua, or debuting on a Broadway stage.

And, what about my childhood puppy, Holly? Would she still be around six, seven, years from now? She was already ten. Dad had given her to me for my eighth birthday.

"You're not promising," Lilly prodded.

I ruffled her hair. "I won't peek. I promise. You be good, okay, Squirt?" My nickname for her when we played "finding Nemo" in the backyard had always made her giggle before. She had a toy squid she'd squirt at me when I couldn't locate the rubber Nemo she'd hide.

I practically sprinted out of the waiting room, afraid I'd changed my mind about leaving. I was already late for the bank meeting, and Sarah was going to be livid.

"Hey! Wait up!" Pastor Perry ran after me. "I need to drive you back."

I'd forgotten.

I was silent most of the walk to his van.

"You haven't had much sleep lately?" He pointed

to the pouches under his own eyes. He must have been wondering about the suitcases under my lower lids.

"Late nights. Too many early mornings."

"As long as it's not nightmares keeping you awake." He chuckled.

"Actually, I've had a few." I remembered the dreams that had jolted me up. Always the same intruder. The robbery had shaken me up more than I admitted. "But they're nothing. Just fears we all have acting out. Or maybe the Chinese takeout for dinner." I giggled.

He stopped when we got to the van but just stood without opening the door. "Sometimes dreams may mean more than just the spicy takeout. The subconscious mind is aware of things you or I could easily overlook. What did you dream about?"

Just what I needed: an interrogator. "Stupid stuff."

"Nothing's stupid if it scares you."

"You believe dreams come true?" I didn't mean to remind him of his daughter and hated myself for having blurted that.

"Some." He sounded sad. He opened the doors, and we drove off.

"Isn't that like New Age stuff? Believing that dreams can come true?"

"You'd be surprised to learn the Bible has people dream dreams that turned out just as they saw it in their sleep. More than a half-dozen incidents. Sometimes, they were warnings from God."

Right. "Pilate's wife."

"Not specifically hers. But, there were others."

"So, did they heed the...warnings?"

"Usually."

His white van was passing the El Camino now. I glanced out the window and noticed we were about three blocks away from Stay Fit. "What happened when these Bible characters *didn't* heed?"

"They weren't just Bible characters. They were real people, like you and me. The Bible is, after all, history, too. You want to guess what happened to them?"

I shrugged. "They got...struck by lightning?"

He barked out a laugh. "There was Joseph, Jacob's son. Heard of him?"

"The son with the multi-colored coat?" We'd done the musical at school, and I'd been one of the props. Lame.

"Joseph was betrayed by his ten older brothers and sold to the Egyptians as a slave. Years later, God gave him dreams that brought him out of slavery. And, because he heeded the warnings, and the pharaoh at the time did, too, the residents of that region were delivered from famine and death. You can read for yourself in the book of Genesis."

I nodded. "Cool story." At least Sarah was going to deliver me to wealth. By that time, we'd already arrived at the fitness place, and it was already past ten.

"Like I said, these are not just stories. The Bible is also a history book. Events are verified by other non- Bible-believing historians."

"Like non-Christian historians?"

"Several. Tacitus, Thallus, and a few others. They lived in the first century."

History. One of my favorite subjects. I nodded. "Thanks for the ride. And the history lesson."

"Sure. Call me, and we can continue on the dream topic."

"Thanks. That was insightful. Might help me some."

I slammed the door a bit harder than I meant to and hustled toward my Mini Cooper. I turned to wave at him. Pastor Perry was staring at me as he sat in his white van. He wore a frown.

How could I, a sane, almost straight-A student, take my nightmares seriously? I could understand someone wanting to kill Sarah, hence our escape plan. But, who'd want to injure me? I had no money, no gorgeous hunk hanging on to my arm waiting to lavish me with all sorts of gifts, or for any female to be jealous over, no multi- colored coat, not even a career, as far as my brother was concerned. Nothing. *Nada*, as they say it here in Spanish- speaking California.

Actually, I'd had dreams that had come true

before. Twice. Although, some might argue these were coincidences.

When my mother had that late-term miscarriage five years back, I'd dreamt I saw a shadow enter her bedroom consecutively for five days. On the sixth day, Mom had stayed in her room the entire afternoon, crying. (I'd heard her through the cracks under her bedroom door.)

Later that evening, Dad had broken the news about her miscarriage: something about Mom's age—she'd been forty-five, and the dangers of pregnancies late in life.

Another time had been when my first and *only* boyfriend, Drew Sanders, had gone to Russia on a gymnastics competition. I'd dreamt he'd have an accident while flipping on the rings. I'd casually mentioned the dream to him but he'd thought nothing of it, and I'd also attributed it to the fact I was going to miss him.

While in Moscow, Drew's hand had slipped, and he'd lost his hold. He'd fallen and broken his spine. His parents had taken him to New York City and to all sorts of specialists, and I never saw him again.

Last I'd heard from our mutual high school buddies, via Facebook, Drew's whole life revolved around therapies. He'd never even contacted me. I always wondered why and held hopes he would someday.

Still, those were not valid examples. Their probabilities worked. However, the likelihood someone would actually find me worth harming ran slim. Or so I felt.

❖Chapter Twenty-Seven❖

THE ICU REQUIRED cell phones be turned off, and I'd forgotten to switch it back on when I'd breezed out of there. So I hurriedly turned it on. As I drove, it started buzzing. It was Sarah.

"Where are you?" She sounded flustered.

"I'll just meet you at the bank. Something came up." I'd driven down the block.

"What?"

"I'll explain later."

"I've broken all my nails punching your number. At least pick up your phone."

"I'm sorry."

"Have you forgotten your clothes and stuff you have to change into?"

It *had* slipped my mind. I had to transform into the new "me," which needed to look as "un-me" as possible so that when I did the bank interview the interrogating officers wouldn't think Sarah and I looked in any way alike.

The basic idea was to present myself as

Humpty Dumpty. Then, when Sarah turned into Brianna O'Mara and got fingerprinted as me, it would be easier for us to switch identities and fool the bankers—even their cameras, if it came to that. It wouldn't do for anyone there to register subconsciously that we looked similar to begin with, Sarah had stressed. I had no idea how Sarah was going to pull off looking pudgy. She was thinner than a beanpole.

"I'll—I..."

"I'll—I, what?" she snapped. "I'll bring your clothes with me, and you can change at the McDonald's two blocks from Fremont Bank."

"I know where that is."

"Don't be late. Eleven is the appointment at Fremont. They're not like a Bank of America. They close at noon, sharp. I'm already driving there." It was ten forty.

"I'll be there."

I slammed my foot on the accelerator, breezed down Willow and Middlefield, and swung a right at the traffic light toward the Hooper Street McDonald's. No parking was available in the public lot next to the bank. As I backed up into a tight spot between two Ford trucks, I saw a yellow Corvette whiz past behind me on Main Street. Had it come from the parking lot I'd pulled out of?

Why would Keith, assuming it was him, be here? Was he suspecting something and tailing me? I wouldn't put it past him to spy on me and make me look bad in front of my parents. My stomach twisted, and I had the PMS- cramped feel in my abs. A few Tums would have helped.

But then, it could be that Keith just had a client appointment, I reassured myself and took a few deep breaths to steady my heart beat. What excuse could I give him for not being at work at this hour, if he saw and stopped me? Right after I'd taken leave to see Dad, too.

Sarah had never met anyone from my family, but she'd seen photos of Keith in my cell phone camera gallery, where I stored some pictures of my relatives. Unfortunately, I'd shown Keith shots of her, too. Would he recognize Sarah and interrogate her? It was crucial I got to her before he spotted her. And, being the chatty sort, would he have told her of our dad's condition if he'd already recognized and stopped her?

A sudden sharp rap on my driver side window jolted me.

"Hey!" Sarah's worried face peered at me. Maybe Keith *had* told her.

She stepped back and jerked her chin at me. Was she annoyed?

"I just got here," I said.

"Oh, good. I thought I'd kept you waiting." I stared at her and realized I'd never heard her come close to being considerate, especially about timing. This switch deal must have been weighing heavy on her.

She had on a bright yellow pants suit, with a light blue, silky blouse peeking from under the nipped-waist blazer. Some modern Chanel. The same outfit but a size bigger awaited me at the apartment. She'd purchased all this the day before.

Sarah went on, saying, "I got your stuff." She shoved two large brown paper bags, the sort they gave out at Bloomingdale's, at my face. Faded blue jeans with rhinestones on the pockets and a claret-colored, loose- knitted blouse were inside one. The blouse was going to make me dumpy. And I was to use my sneakers with the outfit.

We hurried toward McDonald's, Sarah tottering on her five-inch, black heels. Her pants covered most of the stiletto. I had the same style and color waiting at home, but thankfully mine only had a two-inch stack. No way could I pull off that high of a perch without stumbling. Would anyone at the bank notice the slight height variation in our shoes? Someone with a keen eye for fashion might.

The lunch crowd hadn't started so we had the restrooms to ourselves. The jeans fitted fine, if a tad short, but the blouse hung like a sack.

"Perfect," Sarah said.

She'd also brought one of those weighted waistbands I had to secure around my middle to give me a more pudgy look, so the bank officials would remember me as rotund. This would make it easier to emulate me when Sarah had to pass off as Brianna, the pudgy-in-the- midsection girl. We'd also agreed on me wearing glasses, so when she was me, she'd put on a pair of far-sighted spectacles that would make her eyes bigger and more like mine.

My years of stage work had prepared me for our biggest challenge: makeup to widen and flatten my cheeks so my face looked rounder. Highlights on the upper bridge of my nose to give me a less chiseled look. If anyone noticed anything at all about me, they'd believe I had a moon face to go with the rotund torso.

I applied some dark tones to hollow out Sarah's cheeks, giving her face a slimming effect. My real face shape was more oval and bonier. I already had my hair in a ponytail and that would work fine, since Sarah's was bobbed and rounded at her shoulders. We calculated that by the time we finished with the first phase of paperwork, it would be noon. That would give us time to get to our apartment, and we would switch hair color.

After trying the hairpieces, we'd both agreed they screamed of fake. So, we'd tossed the wig idea. Thank goodness for the wonders of dyes. I'd need to cut my length, too, since my hair was quite a bit longer than Sarah's and too voluminous. She'd get away with light- brown hair extensions, which we would sweep into the ponytail.

"It's a good thing Jackson won't be there later when we switch," I told her.

She nodded.

Anyone looking on would have thought we were

getting ready for a party, with all the makeup brushes and contour sticks that went back and forth between Sarah's face and mine. Twenty minutes later, which meant we were already late, no one could have said that Sarah and I looked remotely alike, except that if anyone studied us closely enough, it was obvious we had an inch of makeup on.

"Where are you parked?" I asked.

"That big lot behind here." She looked at the mirror and smacked her lips together. They were painted a bright red, which made her lips look as if bumblebees had stung them.

"Did you see a yellow Corvette come out from there?"

"Yellow what?" She asked dumbly as she stuck on false eyelashes. When it was my turn to become Sarah, I'd have to secure the fake lashes on, too. For now, I just had my real, scanty ones.

But how could she not have seen that flashy-looking car? A cold wave brushed my arm. "I think it passed by our apartment building earlier. You didn't happen to see it?"

She frowned at me, as if annoyed. "I was boxing my stuff, not staring out windows. Were you expecting your *brother* to visit? I thought you were practically estranged from him."

So, she remembered Keith drove a Corvette. "Nothing to be agitated about. He's not the visiting-sister kind of bro. I just thought…. My mind's been playing tricks on me." Perhaps the lack of sleep, the stress, the fear, the nightmares had conspired to conjure imaginary images in my brain. Minds had been known to crack under less pressure.

"Forget it," I said.

"You have to stay focused or we won't be able to pull this off. We have to hustle. We're already late. Jackson will kill me."

What would Jackson say about her makeup? Or, was he used to her dramatics? Probably.

We scurried out of McDonald's just as a wave of office workers breezed in and almost knocked my Bloomingdale's brown bag out of my grasp at the exit. My car was closer, so we tossed the evidence of our scheme in the trunk and headed toward Fremont Bank about thirty yards away.

"Remember, try not to say too much," Sarah warned me. "And you have this habit of pushing your hair behind your ears, even when there's nothing falling over your face. If you did it a few times, I could imitate that."

"Sure." I'd been practicing raising my eyebrows as a manner of accenting, and Sarah would imitate this, too, when she "became" Brie. Something extraordinary like that would be a subconscious hook for people who noticed us to recall and identify us as unique. When they saw Sarah (as me) and noticed the eyebrow-raising thing, they'd psychologically equate this with Brianna O'Mara. At least, I hoped they would.

But what if we were caught? Could we be

charged for switching identities? I never got the chance to research the penalties of us being caught.

❖Chapter Twenty-Eight❖

WHEN I STEPPED through the wooden double doors of Fremont Bank, my breath stuck in my throat. A long Verde marble counter greeted us at the right side, and a booth with a mahogany desk, the Victorian kind with scrolled feet, sat to the left. On a dark brown leather club chair next to the scrolled-feet desk sat a suited man with one leg crossed at the knee. From his profile he looked about fortyish, with a thick head of brown, wavy hair, peppered with silver at the temples.

Opposite him, on the other side of the desk, sat a lady with a black, double-breasted suit made of a soft silk-wool blend: expensive but typical, no-nonsense, "try to impress" banker's style, Sarah termed it as we walked in.

The lady with the banker suit had the whitest blonde hair I'd ever seen. Maybe dyed. I couldn't say for sure. Her name tag said, "Marlene Stefford, Branch Manager, Executive Vice-President."

Blondie Marlene stood and offered her hand toward Sarah as she and I sashayed to the desk.

Jackson—at least, I guessed he was Jackson—whirled around and smiled broadly at us as if we'd just hit the jackpot. And maybe that was how I felt then.

I nervously glanced up at the bank camera focused on us. *What was I getting myself into?*

"And, you must be the lovely Brie. We meet at last." Jackson's Tennessee drawl was even more pronounced than it had been on the phone.

"Nice to meet you." I shook his hand. He had a soft grip. Surprising for a wide-shouldered man, and brawny, too—probably from all the golf.

"Heard much about you." He jerked his chin at Sarah, who stood grinning, showing her even teeth. This was part of the act for me to follow when I was her. Jackson wouldn't be around later, or there would be no way we could pull this off. He'd recognize I wasn't Sarah and vice versa if he was there. Sarah had apparently convinced him he wasn't needed later. He had other clients to tend to, anyway.

"Good things about me, I hope, Mr. Anderson," I said. I pushed invisible hair behind one ear.

"Nothing but the best," Jackson said.

Would he bring up our telephone conversation? Sarah seemed oblivious enough about it, but I never could tell with her. She tended to keep mum about certain things, especially things of which she didn't approve.

The transfer paperwork went smoothly;

Marlene Stefford, with the help of her underling, a Garrot Darcey, who didn't look remotely like Jane Austen's Mr. Darcey, shuffled papers back and forth between them.

This Mr. Darcey had beady eyes, nose beaked like a toucan, and he had the habit of making sure the stacks of paperwork in front of Sarah to sign had their corners squared up, all the while looking over his shoulders as if he expected some bandits to ambush us. It was disconcerting to watch him.

Yellow sticky notes were pasted on each page near the line Sarah was to autograph. Whenever Garrot Darcey added more piles for her signature I kept lifting my eyebrows in feigned surprise so he would notice this eyebrow trait. He kept grinning at me, yellow teeth and all. I hoped he wouldn't discern any of my peculiar natural mannerisms and find them missing when Sarah took my place. She didn't have the acting background I had, although during our practice at home I thought she was quite good—better than I'd given her credit for. If we got caught with our switch, would the bank officers call the cops?

My gaze shot up to the camera again. These days, it was hard to hide anything with technology. If they blew up our images, could they tell subtleties? And, if it came to it, and my parents were called to identify me, would they wonder why my makeup was about two inches thick?

Concentrate.

Sarah had Jackson to bail her out, but with my dad hospitalized, I couldn't add to my mother's burdens. And forget about Keith.

A knot formed in the pit of my stomach. Was it too late to pull out of this? I was worried for my dad. Sarah had insisted I turn off my phone. What if there were an emergency at the hospital?

"That's it for now." Marlene stood abruptly and gathered the signed documents; her sharp nails, red like blood, scratched the papers as she sorted the stack. Definitely the fashionista sort.

I dragged my feet to hide them under my swivel seat. With her heels, Sarah stood at least two inches taller than I did, but, would Marlene realize later that the "new" Brie was actually shorter than this present one? It might not be so easy to fool her.

Marlene cleared her throat. "Ladies, why don't you grab a quick lunch and be back here in forty-five minutes?"

I glared at Sarah, who looked as horrified as I felt. Forty-five minutes? That wasn't enough time to get my hair cut at the salon. I was sure I was going to get an ear-full from the hairdresser about having too much hair, as it was. And no way she could rush through this.

After the cut, I had to dye the massive thing at home—a just-in-case measure, as we didn't want the cops to know about the hair-color, should they get a hold of the hairdresser. Then, we'd need to switch make-up, re-dress, gather enough breath to calm ourselves, and arrive back here. Even theater performances didn't demand such speedy changes.

Sarah stood, a fake smile plastered on her face. She thrust her hand out at Marlene for a handshake. "Thanks for everything so far. But, the bank agreed on us coming back here at three and I have a prior engagement before that."

Marlene, her face as cold as the Verde marble counter, pumped Sarah's hand. "I have an emergency meeting I have to get to that is mandatory for all the Vice Presidents in the branch. Is there a way you can rearrange your engagement?"

"It's set in stone," Sarah said.

"An appointment with the hair stylist, maybe?" Marlene smirked and winked at me, as I pushed my seat back and stood next to Sarah. My gut twisted.

Was that a wild guess? My heart popped up to my throat—that roller-coaster feeling when the car took that first plunge. How were we going to pull off our plan in forty-five minutes?

Jackson stepped in front of Sarah. "My client needs the time to sort her mind before the final papers get signed. As you can see, this is a big decision and demands serious thought. I believe the law requires at least a three-hour window on these matters due to the legal ramifications."

Such lawyerly jargon. It sounded as if Jackson knew of our plan. Perhaps a part of it.

"Oh." Blondie glanced up at the clock on top of

the arched entry and held out her hand, palm facing us, as if to apologize. "I'll make a quick call and sort this out. Maybe my assistant V.P. can sit in for the signing. I believe Miss McIntyre met Mr. McGraw when he set up her account."

Sarah's face slipped a few shades paler. Things were not going as smoothly as we'd hoped.

❖Chapter Twenty-Nine❖

Seconds dragged to minutes as I
looked from Marlene to Sarah to Jackson. This would
be devastating to our plan. Darcey had already
stalked off with the stacks, presumably to double-
check everything. Ninety-nine million was a lot of
money.

Sarah shot Jackson a glare, and as if he
understood her unspoken words he said, "I'm afraid
the law requires that the banker's representative
present for the first signing be there at the second,
as well." He grinned at Blondie. Was he in on our
scoop?

Marlene said, "Why don't you ladies take a break,
and I'll check on these details? Let's keep the original
appointment, then. I'm sure my directors will be
able to excuse me from the emergency meeting." She
smiled sweetly. "The bank holds the McIntyre
account in high regard, so I'm sure I could be here
at three." With that, she swiveled on her stilettos
and rushed off, her heels *click-clicking* on the
marble flooring.

That was close!

Sarah tugged at my arm. "You go off first."

I nodded, waved at Jackson, who appeared anxious to talk with Sarah, and scooted out the door. It was only at my car that I realized that, like an idiot, I'd left my yellow duffle at the bank, so I quickly scampered back to get it.

As I rounded the corner, I heard Jackson's southern twang.

He and Sarah stood a few steps away from where I was hidden behind a pillar. They were on the side of the bank near the parking lot. I meant to tell them I needed to retrieve my bag, but I stopped myself when I saw Sarah's hand. She had taken a bundle out of her LV backpack. It looked like a brown bag used for packed lunches, similar to the ones she'd handed me on two occasions. She passed it to Jackson. What was in it?

Jackson opened it and peeked inside while Sarah looked over her shoulders stealthily, and almost caught me peering,. Fortunately, I'd already pulled my head back behind the pillar. I'd never seen her so worried-looking.

"Remember, don't call me," Sarah said quietly. "I'll contact you if I need further help."

"Nice working with you." Jackson must have walked away in a hurry as his cowboy boots pounded on the asphalt.

It sounded like Jackson was in on our plan. Why

had Sarah not told me this? A tight knot formed in my throat. After all I'd agreed to, Sarah still couldn't tell me? She must not realize that, despite what I had to gain from her inheritance, I was losing something of myself, too. What would it have to take for her to trust me as a friend?

I had half a mind to step out and confront her, but scenes weren't my thing, and I figured if we were to build a life together as sisters in crime, so to speak, this might be a counterproductive approach. I would find a tactful way to bring up her lack of trust. Perhaps on our plane ride.

When I peeked again, Sarah had reached her forest green Jag. Perhaps Jackson wasn't just her attorney, looking out for her interests. He could just have been her stooge who enjoyed her wads of cash. I lost respect for this so-called lawyer who could be bought so easily. And, in some way, I was disappointed with Sarah, too. But, was I any better?

Near the bank's mahogany desk, just as I'd left it, I saw my yellow duffel. Who'd pilfer something so cheap in such a posh institution, right? It's a good thing no one tossed it in the trash.

During the short drive to the salon, Jackson's words rang in my ears. "Nice working with you." She'd paid him off. I couldn't—shouldn't—corner her and force her to confess. She'd think I was spying…which I guessed I was.

The haircut went smoothly enough, despite the hairstylist complaining about the double dose of hair I had. She'd joked that she should charge me twice. I hoped this wouldn't make me memorable to her if for any reason she was questioned later. It was a salon I'd never visited so as to keep the anonymity. I even paid cash.

"Hey!" Sarah greeted me when I stepped back into our apartment. She already had her hair wrapped in a towel, her color work already completed. "What took you so long?"

"I, uh....." I held out my bag. "I misplaced...."

"Never mind. Let's hurry." She headed toward my bedroom's bathroom, where she'd laid out all the dyeing agents on the bathroom sink. L'Oreal products. Would my hair color take the dye and turn my shade to look exactly like Sarah's rich red? I had my concerns but kept my mouth shut. Sarah already seemed nervous.

"Like it?" I swung my shorter hair about and pretended I was reveling in our adventurous plot, even though the bank scene I'd spied on still played in my head like a Cineplex set on auto. How to approach Sarah without offending her? She was touchy about so many things.

"We only have a little over an hour," Sarah said. "Do you mind sitting so I can start this?"

"And exactly how long have you been coloring people's hair?"

"Just because I go to the salon doesn't mean I

can't do it."

"Really?"

"No need to be so sarcastic."

"Have you actually taken classes for this?" I picked up the coloring tube and scanned the instructions.

"Maybe I have. Maybe I'm smarter than you think."

"Sorry. I just don't want to end up with green hair. It *could* look awkward."

She slipped her hands into the surgical-like gloves and pretended to choke me, then started to attack the tubes. I glanced nervously at her as she mixed the solutions.

"Stop looking so nervous, will ya?" she said. "You'll give the game away."

Under her charge, I could end up as a carrot top, or have my hair turn fuchsia or some ghastly pukey color, like puce, for instance.

I sat on the blue plastic molded chair that was part of our soon-to-be-donated dining set and draped the black towel she'd brought in for the process over my shoulders. I practically held my breath through the entire procedure.

"Gawd, woman," Sarah said. "Could you please breathe? You're turning purple and it doesn't match your new hair color."

How she could joke at a time like this?

Later, when we looked at the full-length mirror

in my walk-in closet, I stepped back involuntarily. It was remarkable. We'd taken "before" pictures with my phone, and I'd have bet my last dime that afterward even Keith might have had trouble telling us apart at first glance. Especially when we put in the colored contacts. No wonder Peter Salazar had commented on how alike we looked. Perhaps he had been studying my features and had noticed this more than anybody else.

Although our coloring was different, our eyes, nose and the curve of our upper lips were almost identical. Sarah was probably uncomfortable that she didn't look as unique as she'd like to have been.

For several minutes, Sarah and I practiced some of the mannerisms we'd agreed upon, and she did a believable rendition of the "me" in the bank. She flicked hair that wasn't there away from her cheeks and once in a while chewed on her nails, which by this time were chipped and bitten like mine had been minutes ago. Now I had on acrylic nails, red as the devil's pitchfork, and too long to be practical for any house chores, or doing any sort of barista work.

"Will Marlene notice our change?" I asked as we packed up the hair dyes and stuffed them into black garbage bags, which we intended to toss on our way to the bank. Marlene had seemed like a person conscious of fashion.

"If you stopped looking so nervous, we might get away with this."

I sighed.

She punched my arm. "We can practice our facial expressions a bit more." She stuck her tongue out at me.

During the practice time, though, I thought about Dad. Was he out of his coma? He'd be sad I wasn't there when he came to. My mother must have been furious if she'd tried to contact me and found my phone switched off. Sarah insisted I stayed focused, and I had no choice but to heed her.

"When this stint is done you can call your parents one last time," she reminded me when I took my phone and glanced at the blank screen. "Everything comes with a price, Brie. We can't risk mistakes. Understand?" she continued when I bit my lower lip—something I reminded myself *not* to do, now that I was Sarah for the moment.

"Maybe I can call them when we get to a more rural place—like the Bahamas."

"For someone who wants to get away from them, you're sure acting dorky."

I nodded glumly. Easy for her to say, she didn't have a dad in ICU.

❖Chapter Thirty❖

Just as I disarmed the alarm by the front entry to leave, the doorbell rang. Sarah gave me a furious stare, as if I were to blame for this surprise visitor. I wondered if it was Keith. It would be hard to explain our looks. I peeked through the keyhole, and my breath left me with a jolt, so loudly that I wondered if our visitor heard me. I turned to Sarah and jerked her into the kitchen while the doorbell kept *ding-donging*.

"It's Pastor Perry!" I whispered, even though no one outside our door could hear us.

"Why's he here?" Sarah's cheeks flushed, even beneath the pale ivory foundation I'd caked on her face.

"I don't know. He's nosey."

"We can ignore him."

"He's persistent. But he can't see us. He'll suspect something."

I peeked out the kitchen window and saw his clunky Dodge van on Emerson Street. "Take off your ponytail, and open the door. Tell him I'm not home.

See what he says," I whispered, again.

My stomach churned and tightened. Why was Pastor Perry here? Was it more bad news about Dad? And what if he'd noticed my car in the garage? "He's never met you, so he won't suspect anything." I was banking on the hope Pastor Perry wouldn't mention Dad's condition to someone he didn't know. I kept my fingers crossed.

While Sarah was occupied with Pastor Perry, I planned to peek at my cell phone and check for messages.

"We don't have time." Sarah glanced up at the clock on the microwave oven and pulled off the hair tie securing her hair and hair extension into a ponytail. She stalked off to the front door, and said in a singsong voice, "Who's there?" Nobody could have guessed she was nervous.

Pastor Perry mumbled something inaudible.

"She's not here. I don't know—she's not due at Starbucks till four."

More mumbling.

"I don't know why she's not answering her phone. Try later."

My gut twisted again, and I pressed my fists against my abs. Maybe some Tums would help. I took the chance to turn on my cell. Maybe they'd been trying to tell me something horrid had happened, and here I was, having a makeover! My Samsung made the usual update sounds to alert me of the many notices I'd missed during the last hours. Probably Facebook notifications. I quickly muted the volume.

"Sure. I'll let her know," Sarah said.

I jiggled the Samsung, hoping stupidly that the shaking would make the phone work faster. When I touched the text icon, I saw Mom had messaged me four times. This was a first for her; she'd never even texted once to me. Each message was short and sounded like a scream.

"Where are you?" Everything was spelled out in full. "We need you here," the next text, sent two minutes later, said.

It must have taken her ages to type all this out, what with her bad eyesight and all.

"Doctor Chen wants you here." Surely, she couldn't have punched in all the words, unless Lilly had texted on her behalf, or maybe, Pastor Perry, himself had done so for her. "Please call as soon as possible."

Not the most telling news. Except Mom seemed desperate.

"Hey!" Sarah's voice literally made me drop the phone and it clattered onto the linoleum floor. "I thought we'd agreed to go dark until after our stint? No distractions, remember?" She pointed to the cell phone, and wagged her bony finger at me.

"What did Pastor Perry say?" I held my breath and picked up my cell.

"He's persistent. I can see why you'd want to get away. From them all." Sarah shoved a fist at me. "He gave you a present."

"What?"

She opened her fist and showed me a small box. "Why'd he give this to you?"

I must really look bad for Pastor Perry to pass me something like this. "Must think I need better sleep." I grabbed the small gift—a box of Sleep Aid.

"He said take only one." Sarah sniggered. "But it's non-habit forming so it's safe."

"Well? What else did he say?"

"You expecting some *other* big news?"

"As a matter of fact, yes. If you don't tell me I'm going to run after him and spoil our plan. I don't care," I practically yelled. From the small kitchen window I saw Pastor Perry walk slowly with his slight limp to his van. His shoulder looked slumped. If I shouted, he'd hear me. Then my life would remain simple, unfulfilled, but I wouldn't have to live like a fugitive.

"No need to get all bent out of shape. Your mom wants you to call. He didn't elaborate. So, what's up with your family?" She went to the window and closed the shutters just as I saw him pull away. It felt as if my old me was pulling away, too, and the new me was strengthening its hold. I shook the feeling away.

"Usual family crisis. Every family has them. Are

we leaving for the bank now?"

Sarah turned and winked at me. "We'd better. Ready to win an Oscar?"

❖ Chapter Thirty-One ❖

AS IT HAPPENED, we were already late. Again.

"Breathe deeply," Sarah said, squeezing my arm as we walked to my Mini Cooper. "Everything will turn out fine."

Would it? A tiny voice whispered in my head. Even if I didn't screw up at the bank, could we get away with this? And if we did, would I live a life of regrets?

Sarah kidnapped my Samsung and reminded me it could be used as a GPS to track us down. There went my chance to ask about Dad. Half of me wanted to scream, "I'm out. Let's stop this, Sarah."

But the voice inside me said it was too late.

On the way there, in my Mini Cooper, with Sarah driving, she lectured me on the importance of anonymity. No Facebook, Twitter, Instagram, or any social media platform—not that I was a social-media junkie, having always guarded my privacy. And, certainly, my Google email had to be deactivated, in case I accidentally commented on YouTube in the future under the account and our whereabouts were traced.

Nothing escaped the government, according to Sarah. Their satellites could pin-point me even to the precise room I was in, she warned.

Worse, I was to hand over my laptop to her before we left for the airport. The K-twins would take it to a tech rehash center that would dismantle both our computers so they could never be traced to us. She'd definitely been reading too much of this conspiracy theory stuff.

As the paperwork progressed at the bank, I worried more and more, and I had to dab my brows a few times. I worried that the sweat would streak my foundation, and my pale coloring would peek out from under the tan makeup I had slathered on my face. *Twice* the contacts made my eyes itchy and I almost rubbed them out. *And* I was sure my fake lashes were already crooked.

Also, I caught Blondie Marlene staring at me but I couldn't be sure, and flashed my gorgeous blood-red nails and acted as "Sarah-ish" as possible. Except for Sarah's obvious annoyance with me for having turned on my phone, nothing seemed to have spoiled our plan.

After the signing, when we trudged back to my car, the red truck I'd noticed in front of our apartment yesterday morning was in the parking lot. I assumed it was the same truck because of its shiny bumper, although red trucks, this one being a Ford, weren't that uncommon. Like a nervous wreck, my heart skipped a beat. Was Jim still looking out for us? Or his partner, Alias? Without my cell phone, I couldn't check to see if Jim had responded since we'd left the apartment.

"Hey," I jerked Sarah's arm toward the red truck. "Could that be Jim's friend? The same one on our street yesterday morning?"

She swiveled her head for a quick glance and hurriedly stepped in the opposite direction, toward where my Mini Cooper was parked. "I didn't pay Jim anything extra to guard us out here in the open, and Uncle Stuart would never do anything that obvious. Too many witnesses."

"So, you don't think that was the same truck?" I wanted to see if she'd confess she'd chatted with the driver that morning, and possibly even kissed him. Or, maybe she'd tell me about the new boyfriend she insisted on keeping secret.

"Did you take the plate number of the truck you saw?" She shrugged and continued walking to my car. "Red trucks aren't exactly pink elephants. Practically one on every corner." She waved at the street.

"Silly me."

Before I slid into the passenger side of the Mini Cooper, I glanced over the black-top of my car. The driver of the red truck wore a Stetson-type hat pulled down over his forehead, as if he were sleeping. Was I being paranoid?

"So," Sarah said, "Excited you have a share in

my trust fund *and* inheritance now?"

Technically, the inheritance hadn't been deposited into the account yet. We still had nine days until the big date. But, the paperwork had been set up, and the Fremont Bank would direct the cache to Swiss Banque Paris once the amount was cleared to go.

After that, transferring the cash to a secured offshore bank located in the Caribbean and with far more privacy clauses should be a cinch. Apparently, nowadays even Swiss banks had to comply with Interpol and international laws that didn't honor privacy, thanks to money-laundering problems.

"Ninety-nine million is quite an inheritance." I yanked the left false eyelash off and tossed it out the window as my car zipped around the bend, away from the bank. Away from my first crime scene.

Sarah gave a short laugh. "Let's hope I don't end up dead, or the cops will pin it on you." She went into hysterics as if her joke was funny.

"What?" How could she make fun about something like that after the burglary?

She went on, "It's easy for them to say you have the motive. Of course, I trust you with my life. Otherwise, I wouldn't have done this."

❖ Chapter Thirty-Two ❖

IN MANY WAYS, I'd entrusted Sarah with mine, too—my insignificant life, with no millions to its credit, but still a life worth living.

"We'd better take extra precautions the next few days," I said. "Maybe get Jim to watch over us." I hoped this would motivate Sarah to say, "Yes. Go ahead, call him," or, "Let's ask Pete how we can reach him."

Sarah said, "Nah! We'll be fine. We have the alarm to warn us. And Uncle's not the sort to work with haste. Now that he's failed in his first attempt, he'll wait for a bit. Space things out, just in case the burglary gets traced to him. He doesn't know we haven't gone to the cops, so he's going to lay low. That's how he's been covering his tracks. Patience." Her eyes shifted to the ceiling for a split second and she added, "Like a cobra in the rushes calculating for the precise moment to strike."

The hair on my arms stood on ends. "You mean, that wasn't the first time he tried to hurt you?"

She nodded. "I assure you, it'll be his last. He'll

never find me after we disappear."

How could she be sure? If Stuart McIntyre was closely connected to some dark world of assassins and espionage, as Sarah had insinuated, he'd have the resources to trace her movements. As long as she was alive, he'd surely be keeping tabs on her. I shivered, even though that April afternoon was warm that spring.

"Can I have my phone back for a bit?"

She rummaged in her LV and held up my Samsung, then pretended to pass it to me but suddenly snatched her hand away before I could grab the phone.

"Stop teasing," I said.

"You realize our relationship has to be based on trust. Before I hand this to you..." She waved the phone about. "Perhaps there's something you want to confess?" She raised an eyebrow.

It occurred to me what she'd done. "You're one to talk about trust. You read my text messages, didn't you?"

"If you have nothing to hide, why be so secretive?"

I could say the same, but I bit my tongue. "It's called privacy." I glared at her. *Fine way to start our oneness. Might be worse than being married.*

"No need to be so edgy. Gawd, Brie, you think I'm some cold-blooded reptile?" Her cheeks flushed tomato- red despite the pale makeup.

"I didn't want you worried. Yes, I should have told you, but I was scared to think about my dad's stroke. What if I leave and never see him again?"

Maybe she couldn't relate because she'd never felt close to her parents, what with boarding schools in England and vacations with her private school friends instead of her family. Plus, her parents had been gone for a while.

"I'll let you see your dad one last time before we vamoose outta here. Tomorrow, we finalize the furniture removal. The K twins arranged that for me—for a few bucks extra, of course."

"Do they know about us moving?"

"Naturally. I bragged about us taking a trip to Hawaii for R and R. They just rolled their eyes. If the cops questioned they'd think we went there, but we'll be out of the States by then."

I still worried about the fake passports she'd arranged for us. What if Interpol got wind we were carrying fake IDs? That was a federal *and* an international crime.

She handed me the phone. I checked the messages and saw Mom, and now also Lilly, had texted me three more times each.

"How do we get to Switzerland? Won't the cops know to check our movements? They have Interpol at their disposal," I said, my eyes scanning the urgent text messages. Somehow, each text felt like a stab to my heart. Was it too late to back out?

"All taken care of. I bought two tickets to Hawaii, and also two to Mexico City. The United tickets to Hawaii are just decoys. The Mexico tickets bear our fake names. Sienna Smith—that's you." She winked at me. "And Taylor West—that's me. Like your new name? I even have fake California driver's licenses to go with these." She groped in her LV and fished out two IDs, one with my face on it. "I'll keep them safe for the both of us."

"So, who's inheriting the Hawaii tickets?" It would have been fun to bake in the Maui sun. I'd heard about the island's clear waters, warm winds, and the heavenly snorkeling. Maybe we'd get there once all this was behind us.

"I sold the tickets on e-Bay. There was a company that buys purchased tickets. Can you believe it? I don't even know how they'd change the names, underground market and all, but that would work the cops for a bit till we're safely out of US airspace. Besides, it gives the FBI a chance to clamp down on these illegal activities. Think of it as us doing the American public a civic duty, a service to rid society of evil corporations."

Right! What did I get myself into?

"Stop being a snort bowl," she said, and waved at me as if I were a mosquito buzzing too close to her.

"Snort bowl?"

She pretended to dig her nose and made a face. "C'mon. You'll love the travel. We fly to Mexico tomorrow afternoon then connect to London. Both flights are on Mexican Air. I found out their computer system isn't up to date, so the inefficiency works in our favor. Also, Brian Susman—that's the guy I got the Mex Air tickets from— assured me that the Mexican staff is more open to… monetary incentives, shall we say? And Brian's contacts have taken care of covering our tracks."

I swallowed hard. Some things she said didn't register. "Who's Brian Sussman? Is he trustworthy?"

"I met him years back when I went to that English boarding school. He's not one to run to the Bobbies, I can tell you that. Too many skeletons in his family's closet."

I didn't dare ask whose skeleton, so I just sighed.

"So, make sure you're set to leave tomorrow morning."

I jerked so hard my head hit the ceiling of the car. "Did you say *tomorrow morning*? That's too soon. I thought we had a couple more days. I can't move that fast." The car squealed when she braked suddenly as we reached my assigned parking spot below the apartment building.

"No need to panic. Ga-wd! Besides, it's not like you have a long list of pals to bid farewell to."

Ouch! "You said we…"

"Let me explain." She shook her head. "My contact in London can house us for a day or two so nothing goes on black and white, and we won't have to use credit cards." She swiveled in her seat

185

and faced me squarely. "Stop looking so dismal. Gawd!"

Why'd she keep on saying "God?" The very being I'd been trying to avoid. Could God even help me, if I wanted out?

I grabbed my LV backpack, the spanking-new one Sarah had gotten me, together with my old duffel she'd used when at the Bank, heaved myself off my seat, and slammed the Mini Cooper door a tad too forcefully, making the whole car rattle. I was going to miss my tiny British car— although, if I ended up in the UK, it'd be easy enough to replace it and blend with the English public.

I'd read that it was a snap to get around in London: hop on the Underground, and I could even get over to France and practice my miserable French. But, my dad had bought me the Cooper, and it felt like the last string I had attached to him. Maybe I should never have agreed to this plot. Was this worth a gazillion bucks? Still, it was too late to back out.

As if reading my thoughts, Sarah ran after me and pulled my arm. "You're just having buyer's remorse. It's common. Trust me. You'll feel better once we're on that plane tomorrow."

I shrugged her hand off and continued my pace. "Whatever." Lilly's text had said Dad was better. Still, I'd wanted to see him, to say good-bye face to face, even though, technically, he wouldn't know it was farewell. I hoped I wouldn't break apart.

❖ Chapter Thirty-Three ❖

QUICKLY, I CHANGED back to my regular outfit, peeled off the false nails that would have made it impossible to drive, and scrunched up what was left of my hair. This way, the dark-red dye wouldn't look so obvious.

Quitting Starbucks went easily enough. Nobody commented on the variation in my hair shade or its length. Pony-tailing helped it not look too obviously different. Nobody cried buckets at the idea of not seeing me there again. And they'd called themselves my friends. The manager, Jane Brown, didn't even seem interested when I handed her the resignation form.

"Have a good one," she hollered as I gathered my things to leave.

Sarah had insisted I come home early to pack items I'd really want to have for always.

"In case you feel homesick," she'd said, winking.

I slipped Lilly's birthday card to me into a side pocked and then sorted through photos, cards, those kinds of portable memorabilia, and a few choice items of clothing I'd insisted on keeping—a bridge to my past. The rest would be donated to the Salvation Army. I got Rosco, the old teddy bear Dad had given me when I'd turned seven, and hugged it. It was something to remember Dad by. I could even smell him in it, as if Rosco stored all the fragrance of my childhood in its faded brown body. That's the thing with scents, they can cut through time and space and transport a person to a past forgotten.

Sarah stepped into my bedroom and snatched my bear from my suitcase when I tossed it in. She shook her head, her eyes wide.

"This?" She dumped my bear back into my luggage.

Someone who got thousands of dollars of stock certificates for her seventh birthday wouldn't understand the value of a cuddly stuffed animal. While I'd been at Starbucks, she'd Fed-Exed the stock certs out to a London address—she didn't elaborate on it. All under more false names, naturally.

I could tell from her mannerisms that something was upsetting her. "The K twins just texted me. They want us to dismantle at least one of the beds so they can quickly take things down for curbside pickup tomorrow."

"The Salvation Army can't dismantle for us?"

"Something about labor laws—they can only disassemble one bed per unit. I even offered to pay and the lady was horrified. We can take yours apart, and you can sleep on your rug." She pointed to the small rectangular splash of floral carpet I had in front of my bed—my attempt to cheer up my room. We'd donate the rug, too.

"Forget it." Of course, it would have to be *my* bed that had to come apart.

"Okay, sleep on the couch, then," she quickly added. "It's only for *one* night."

Come to think of it, she didn't look too happy about it, either. Maybe she had compassion for me after all. Sarah couldn't sleep unless she was reposed on a bed like Cleopatra, complete with goose-down duvets and surrounded by about a dozen pillows.

I sighed. "Fine, I'll relegate myself to the sofa. By the way, you sure you paid Jim?" I asked. There must have been a reason he was avoiding me. At least, that was what I felt.

"Taken care of. Why?" Did Sarah sound worried? It occurred to me that the brown bag of something she'd passed to Jackson could have been meant for Jim. Maybe she'd paid him late, due to her paranoia about not using checks.

"I was wondering why he hasn't returned any of my messages. Thought maybe he's cheesed off with us for not paying." Even Pete had not responded to my last couple of texts when I'd been at Starbucks.

"Quit worrying. Just focus on making this place look like we left for Hawaii." She'd bought bathing suits, and we'd leave the receipts and the price tags in the trash, plus maps of Maui we'd downloaded and printed out. We'd circled spots with red ink to make it seem as if these were the places we planned on visiting, hotels we'd considered and some Sarah had called—for effect, she'd said. We crumpled the maps and tossed them in the trash.

Mr. Yamamoto said he would give us a free cleaning of the apartment and didn't feel he needed to do a final inspection, since he'd received the hefty check, which he apparently had banked on the very day he'd received it. If the cops found the decoy stubs and receipts, provided they looked early enough, they'd be on a goose chase that would buy us time. Hopefully, we'd be in the Caribbean by then.

For their efforts, the K twins would be additionally rewarded with my Mini Cooper. I'd reluctantly handed over my papers to Sarah. She wanted to take care of the nitty-gritty details herself.

"Fine!" I said, flashing my eyes so she'd know my annoyance. I determined to not tell her I was going out that night to visit Dad using my car, which technically was still mine until tomorrow. The strain was taking a toll on Sarah, too. We kept nipping at each other.

For about an hour, we heaved and puffed like the big bad wolf, trying to tear down my twin poster bed with the lilac headboard. My parents had given it to me when I'd reached first grade, and I remembered feeling like a princess when I'd slept in it those first weeks.

Now, with chipped nails and bent screwdrivers, Sarah and I slumped on the floral rug and admitted defeat. I'd never seen her so riled up about anything.

"Can't be done," she said after she'd muttered some expletives.

"We can dismantle *your* bed."

Of course, Miss Princess needed her comfort to sleep. She stared at me as if I'd just suggested she jump off the Golden Gate Bridge.

I said, "Fine. You can sleep on *my* bed. I'll crash on the couch as we'd agreed. And you won't have to feel guilty." This might work out to my advantage.

She looked unsure. "Nah. I'll sleep on the couch."

"You know you won't catch a wink out there and you're going to be a basket case tomorrow. You can barely sleep on your triple-layered down mattress, with a gazillion poufy pillows, and you want to sleep on the *couch*?"

She opened her mouth again but I interrupted. "You've got bags under your eyes. You need the sleep, girl. It's only for a night," I reassured her. "And my bed's comfortable if you pile it up with your dozen poufy clouds."

She nodded slowly, but still looked reluctant. Mighty thoughtful of her—*for once*.

We scooted to her room, and her twin bed came apart in thirty minutes. She'd emptied her drawers, and her Louis Vuitton suitcases sat neatly side by side in front of her walk-in closet.

"You look exhausted," I told her. It was not like Sarah to survive on so little sleep, though it had become a part of my routine. Slight bumps under her eyes had formed and she was antsier than when we'd been at the bank.

"The worst is over," I clapped her on the shoulder, but she shrugged me off. The strain was getting to her, and possibly the physical exertion, too. Taking the bed apart was possibly the most workout outside of a gym for her.

"You'll feel better after a good night's sleep," I said. She flashed me a weak smile.

"Why don't you rest and I'll make you your nightcap."

"Maybe I won't have one tonight."

"What? Don't be insane. You want to have a good sleep so your head will stay clear tomorrow. And you have to get up by six—that's like an unearthly hour for you."

"Maybe I'll take a small sip," she relented, although she didn't sound convinced.

I mused about a plan I'd concocted to remain undetected while visiting Dad. If Sarah caught me it could end our relationship, or at least add to the tension, but I convinced myself that it was a small dastardly deed compared to her deceiving me about Jackson. She might even thank me for helping her slip into such a deep sleep, especially if she'd noticed the bags under her eyes. She was vain that way.

I walked to the kitchen, toward her pitcher of margaritas. She'd been downing one, sometimes two, cupsful every night, with a ring of salt on the rim. The drink helped her sleep better, she'd always said.

With my back to the door, I worked a packet of Sleep-Aid from my jeans pocket and crushed two tiny white pills with a knife on the countertop.

"Can't say you look too hot, yourself," she shot back from the bedroom, when I reminded her about the bags under her lids again.

"We probably both need a nightcap," I said as I drained the last ounce of the margarita into one of the crystal Waterford goblets she always used. I sprinkled the white powder into the margarita, swirled it, and rimmed the goblet with salt granules, just as she liked it.

"Whatever," she said.

"One shot will help you relax." I hoped she'd take it. Of all evenings, I needed her to sleep tight tonight.

❖ Chapter Thirty-Four ❖

LATER, AFTER WE SAID our goodnights, she yelled from my bedroom, "Don't forget to turn on the alarm."

"Will do, boss!" I sat on the sofa and rubbed my scalp with one finger. The dye made my skin itch. My free hand groped the velvet of the cushion. I was going to miss this lousy sofa. My parents had gifted it to me when I'd moved into the apartment. Deep purple velvet chenille fabric. It too, would be donated to the thrift store.

I hugged Rosco, whom I'd taken out of my suitcase for company. I stared into his beady teddy bear eyes.

By nine-thirty, Sarah was snoring in my bedroom. I pressed my ear to the door, and her steady breathing wafted through the gaps. Her margarita and Sleep Aid combo, it seemed, had worked beautifully. Thank you, Pastor Perry.

Wait a few more minutes till she sinks into deeper slumber, hopefully past the point of no return. I paced back to the sofa and lay still like a mummy under my blankets for a minute to gather my wits. When I turned on the stand-up lamp next to me and looked at the microwave oven clock, I realized I'd dozed off. But, I hadn't even had any semblance of those gory dreams of intruders trying to murder us. Peace at last! Perhaps the nightmares were gone for good.

Maybe my luck was turning. Maybe we'd get through the fear we'd suffered that past week, and in two days I'd be in London, then on to Switzerland. The Alps. We'd drink farm-fresh milk, eat meringue dipped into doppled cream, as my brother had done in his travels, and drive through narrow cobbled streets in European cars on the wrong side of the road. And once the inheritance was transferred we could get off to the Bahamas.

Traveling was something I'd envisioned doing, but now I was glad I'd never had a passport, or my fingerprints would certainly be in the system, and the scheme might not have worked. I wondered how Sarah had cleared *her* prints from the database. Brian Susmann might have helped her. I hoped Jim had disposed of our prints as promised. *If I could only get a hold of him.*

It was ten thirty-five, already! How late would the hospital allow visitors, even if I was the doctor's daughter?

I heard something crash in my room. Sarah had probably knocked over my bedside lamp, since she was unfamiliar with the floor plan and arrangements of my furniture. Just my luck if she'd gotten up! She must have been more nervous than I realized, having trouble sleeping despite my concoction. I should have slipped in three tablets instead of two into her margarita.

How was I to escape to the hospital unnoticed? If she barged out and found me gone, I'd have to answer with lies. I wrote a note for her and left it on the coffee table.

"Gone to sleep in bedroom. Don't disturb me. I need the rest." And I scribbled my loopy signature.

Hopefully, she was up only to rush to the bathroom, which thankfully was attached to that bedroom, too—the advantage of having two master bedroom suites in this apartment. I tiptoed to my bedroom, and pressed my ear to the door. Was she still up? Silence inside.

The security system was on. If I turned it off, the beep of the alarm resetting would alert Sarah, especially if she was still awake.

That was when a brain wave hit me. If I could get out through Sarah's window and sneak on the ledge to Mrs. Mott's old apartment, which was a mere twenty feet away, I wouldn't have to use our front door. I was sure my ex-neighbor's sliding door was open. After Mrs. Mott had moved out, a barrage of real-estate agents had shown the apartment. I'd noticed some prospective tenants standing on the balcony, peeking into ours, and then going back in. One complained loudly that Mrs. Mott's old kitchen reeked of stale garlic. Since then, I'd seen agents leave a gap on the slider, presumably to air the place.

I checked the alarm pad and noticed it showed two windows not secured: my bedroom window— Sarah must have forgotten to check before she went to bed— and her bedroom's. That must have been from the night before when I'd entered through her window and later, forgot to turn off the bypass for it.

I dragged some of the sofa cushions into Sarah's old room and pressed the lock button on the knob, so she would think twice before knocking the door and "waking" me. She couldn't guess I'd left.

I grabbed my LV, took a deep breath, and heaved up Sarah's casement, enough so I could scoot out. Of course, now that I was to actually get *on* the ledge, twenty feet seemed quite a distance to tiptoe my way on a six-inch width from here to Mrs. Mott's balcony. Still, it was worth the effort, I convinced myself. Can't take any chances of using my own front door in case Sarah could hear the alarm beep when I opened it. I sucked in my breath.

It's doable, I pacified myself. If I wanted to see my dad one last time I had to do this.

The night air blew upon my cheeks, cool and refreshing, and ruffled my new shoulder-length bob. I'd tie the ponytail extension later in the car so my new hairdo wouldn't announce anything to my family. I'd wear a beanie so the top of my head didn't show the dark-red hair. Hopefully, no one would notice anything different especially since it was night.

With my LV backpack hitched over one shoulder, as I couldn't switch back to my yellow duffel which sat in the bedroom Sarah slept in, I inched toward my goal.

I prayed Sarah had not gone into our kitchen for a glass of milk or was staring at my bedroom window from the bed. Sarah would easily spot me if she sat up in bed. I recalled that man's face peeking in at the window, which even now I could not verify as a dream or reality. He could have been the one who scared Mrs. Mott enough for her to have that initial heart attack.

A deep grumble from some big vehicle revving its engine on the street below almost made me lose my grip, and I tripped over a particularly troublesome foothold. A red truck screamed past, and I tried to blend in with the beige stucco I was clinging to for my life.

Was this the truck from two days ago? The same one that I thought had tailed us to Fremont Bank— Sarah's secret friend? If he'd parked on the street and glanced up at our apartment, my brown jeans and brown hoodie would have been most visible. And, if this was Jim's contact, Alias, supposedly guarding us, he might assume I was the intruder.

The thought that these P.I.s might have guns crossed my mind and for whatever it was worth, I muttered a quick prayer that if they saw me they would think twice and not shoot. That Jim hadn't even bothered to respond to my messages probably meant he'd taken his loot and split, just as Sarah had implied when I'd pestered her again. Everyone had a price, she'd said.

"Gawd, Brie. Give it a break. The man has other clients to take care of, you know?" She'd been visibly annoyed.

Regardless, no one must know I was sneaking out. Not even Jim.

And luck was on my side. I succeeded in getting to the hospital, undetected. But, in doing so, I left Sarah alone.

❖ Chapter Thirty-Five ❖

ACCORDING TO THE NIGHT-duty nurse, Lilly and Mom had been installed in a room next to Dad's. "The door marked 214." Nurse Maisey said when I asked about my family at the desk. "Privilege of your dad being the resident surgeon here," she explained. "No need to look so nervous." She smiled and waved me on.

I nodded and quickened my steps toward Dad's room.

"Brie!" My sister cried out and waved to me from a small lookout as I hurried past a closed door. She had her nose pressed to the glass of the window. It was way past her bedtime.

"Hey! You're up?" I opened the door, and Lilly scooted back to her metal bed and beckoned for me to sit next to her. When I stood over her, she reached out and felt my fake ponytail.

"You cut your hair," she said. The extensions didn't fool her. "It's darker, too." Sharp kid. Even in this dimness, she noticed. Had Nurse Maisey noticed it, too?

I pulled the beanie further down over my ears. I nodded. "How's Dad?"

"He woke up and asked for you, but we couldn't find you. Did you see our messages?"

"Naturally. I was busy helping a friend."

"I got worried when you didn't reply. Mom was, too. So was Pastor Perry. Mom sent him to look for you."

Had Pastor gotten to Stay Fit or Starbucks later and found out I'd quit? I reached into my LV backpack, watching Lilly's face. She was sure to notice this new fashion and suspect something. I pulled out the teddy bear I'd hurriedly shoved into the LV before I'd left and held it out. "Keep Rosco safe for me."

She hugged the bear. "Why's he not safe with you?"

"You're my babysitter. Practice, for when…"

"When what?"

"Never mind. I want Rosco back. So, you keep him, okay? Make sure Holly doesn't maul him to bits. And don't let Holly swallow Rosco's eyes."

She giggled and nodded, brows twisted into a frown. "Pastor Perry wants to talk to you."

"He told you that?"

"I overheard him on the phone. He mentioned something about a nightmare he had about you. Three nights in a row, he said."

My ears perked up. Nightmare? "What did he

say, exactly?"

Lilly tilted her head as if she were scouring the back of her mind. "He dreamed you disappeared."

People had dreams and nightmares all the time. But, why had he dreamed I'd disappeared? He hadn't mentioned anything when we were together in the van, though he'd had that worried frown.

"Anything else?" I kept my eyes on Lilly. She swung her white-socked feet back and forth as she sat up on the edge of her metal bed. Maybe she needed an incentive. She'd always liked those colorful lollypops, and I'd snagged a few from the Fremont Bank teller's jar when I'd slipped in to retrieve my forgotten duffel. Grape was her favorite flavor, and I had two. I dug my hand into the LV. I couldn't remember if I'd transferred it here.

"Nice bag," Lilly said.

"You want it?" I could dump all my stuff into a plastic bag or one of those vomit sacks they always had handy in hospitals: then I could give Lilly my new LV backpack. My going away present. I couldn't imagine walking down the streets of Paris with Sarah, carrying identical bags. But, my fingers, deep in the backpack, wrapped around a phone. A phone in a gel casing, which felt unfamiliar. My Samsung was in a hard case, and I'd left it in the car, as I'd figured the ICU didn't allow such devices. This cell phone wasn't mine: it was Sarah's latest iPhone. I'd snatched Sarah's LV in my haste.

"What's wrong?" Lilly shook my arm, peering at

my face. I felt the blood drain from my neck up and my lips went dry.

"I thought I had some lollypops for you. Sorry."

"You got a new phone, too? You hit the jackpot?" Lilly smirked at me. Smart kid.

"I wish. Hey, I need to use the restroom."

"Sure." Lilly nodded toward an open door that led to the bathroom in the unit.

I dashed inside and locked the door, one hand still clutching Sarah's iPhone. Maybe I could see who she'd called. But, she'd locked it. If I could bypass her password, I could check on that phone number she'd dialed yesterday. Who was it she'd sounded so sultry with on the other line? Red truck guy?

But, no combination I punched into the number pad made a difference, and I couldn't unlock her phone.

I turned her bag inside-out at the sink and examined the articles that clattered into the ceramic white bowl. Sarah's fat Gucci wallet, no doubt with a gazillion credit cards inside. So much for secrecy and anonymity. She'd have to change all the names on the cards and cut these ones up. A lipstick: Chanel Rouge. A mascara with some Italian name I couldn't pronounce, let alone remember to spell. Eye color, "Muted Gray," in a snazzy box by VBN, whatever VBN stood for. Sarah spoke an eclectic language when it came to name brands.

She also had an array of old receipts and papers she'd scribbled on and stuffed inside one of the pockets in her LV. Who'd think a beautiful bag hid so much junk! Except for the makeup and wallet, it was practically a trashcan.

"Brie?" It was my mother's voice. "So glad you finally came, dear." She'd returned to Lilly's room.

"I'll be out soon." The bathroom door was locked, so I wasn't going to be caught red-handed snooping in someone else's bag. I figured with all the trouble I'd already dug myself into, what was this by comparison?

"Dad will be so glad to see you, dearie. He's been asking for you nonstop since he awoke a few hours back."

The guilt trip was beginning. I snapped open the Gucci wallet and studied the cards neatly stacked in the six different compartments. Then my eye caught something, and I shrieked.

"Dearie, are you all right?" my mother asked. I could tell she was in front of the bathroom door. She jiggled the doorknob. "Are you okay?"

"Please, Mother. I'm in the bathroom. Can I have a moment alone?"

"But, you—"

"Please." I stared at the photograph of the man smiling back at me from the photo.

It was not like me to be thrilled, or even overly excited by any hunk of a guy. But, this one made my heart race a million beats a second.

How was this possible?

No explanations popped into my head. Nothing reasonable or logical could possibly explain this. And, it wasn't just his identity. He had one arm in a tight hug around Sarah, his cheek pressed to her forehead. I couldn't see the background. Maybe it was taken at the Golden Gate Bridge, I guessed from the reddish pillars of a structure peeking from the sides in the far distant.

What was Sarah doing with him? My brother? And, why had she kept this a secret from me? Keith, too, why had he pretended he didn't know Sarah? Then I recalled how he'd let it slip by mentioning Sarah's name that first time I'd spoken with him. I'd assumed he'd found out about her from my mother.

This photograph could clarify why he'd gone past my apartment once at least. He must have visited her on his way here to see Dad. It explained his uneasy reaction when I'd questioned him. Was he in on our bank scam? That yellow Corvette at the bank parking lot must have been his. Who was scamming whom? My gut twisted, and I stopped the urge to retch.

I dug and pinched the edge of the photo. Who has photos any more, anyway? Maybe it was taken a few years back. This must be special to Sarah. Were there more incriminating photos in her iPhone gallery?

I wiggled the picture out of the wallet. It felt stuck. On greater scrutiny, I was sure the photo must have been taken years back.

Keith looked different. So did Sarah. Her hair was lighter, almost blondish, streaked, and cropped shorter, which actually suited her face better. Still, there was no mistaking her upturned nose and her thousand-watt smile. I turned the four-by-three-inch snapshot over to check for a date imprinted on the back. It was three years ago. Sarah knew my brother way back then? What game was she playing with me?

I wondered if the person she'd been speaking to in that sultry voice was Keith. She had punched the number as if she didn't want to risk me discovering his number, something I would easily recognize, on her phone. Of course, these were suppositions. The trouble was how to put the photo back without Sarah finding out.

I should just confront her. Taking her bag was just an honest mistake. She must have mine next to her, near the bed. I could demand an explanation, which I resolved to do. If she threatened to expose me for the bank fraud, I'd confess to the authorities and drag her down with me. Better that than run away with a possible psychopath.

What scheme did she have up her sleeve? Maybe Keith had set her up with me for the money, knowing what an idiot I was and that I'd fall for the trap. That must have been it.

Sarah must have known all along I didn't have a passport, had no fingerprints in the system, and had a high motivation to get myself through college and into acting.

My brother must have set it up for her. But how could he? How could Sarah?

So the entire deal was to...what? Steal my identity? With her supposed contacts it must be easier to just buy one of those fake IDs. I could understand her desire to run away and not be found by Uncle Stu or Brother Todd, but why had she involved me?

❖ Chapter Thirty-Six ❖

"Honey?" Mom's voice was right outside the bathroom door again. "Are you okay, sugar?" She jiggled the knob harder.

"Yes, yes. I'll be out."

I scooped out the contents in the sink back into the LV backpack. There was no way I could avoid Mother's eyes on a bag that would cost me a month's salary, at least. Questions were bound to be shot at me. I shrugged the backpack loop onto one shoulder, breathed deeply, and pulled the beanie over my ears more. Time to face the firing squad.

"Sweetie?" There goes the food analogy, again. I unlocked the door and stepped forward.

"Hi, Mom." I bent over and pecked her on the cheek after a quick hug. "Is Keith here?"

"It's been infuriating, trying to get a hold of either of you." Mother shook her head.

"I'm sorry. It's been crazy for me, with work and all."

She sighed and patted the plastic chair by the

foot of the bed. "I even called Stay Fit to find you."

My heart fluttered. Had she spoken to Thao, her contact there, and found out I'd quit? I sat on the edge of the plastic seat, my gut in a knot.

"I must have left," I said.

"Some girl at the sports desk there couldn't even tell me your schedule, kept giving me the run-around. I need to brace you for when you see Dad."

"I heard he's better."

"He's conscious, off and on, but his face is skewed to one side. The nerves on the left," she patted her left check, "were affected by the stroke, Dr. Chen said. But Dad will enjoy hearing your voice."

"He's awake?"

"He can't open his eyes. They don't know why. He nods when you speak to him."

Dad didn't sound as good as I'd hoped. "He's not in a coma anymore, right?"

"He mumbles, here and there. Sometimes it sounds like your name. But, no precise prognosis yet. It takes time. Keep praying for him, sweetie."

I got up from the plastic seat and glanced out the window even though everything was dark out.

"You got a raise, sweetie?" Mother asked. She jerked her chin at the bag on my shoulder.

"Oh, this?" I gestured at the LV. "Sarah got it for me as a present."

"That's generous of her."

Not really. "She's big on giving gifts. Anyway, better go see Dad."

"You be careful, Brianna. People like her don't give presents for nothing." Mother's gray eyes were still on the LV.

Should I mention something, utter some warning? Mother already had so much on her mind. I couldn't possibly burden her more. At eighteen, I was supposed to be a help to my parents, not be a noose around their necks.

"Pastor Perry wanted me to say you can call him any time you need someone to speak with," she said.

Sure. Hey, Pastor. I just committed bank fraud. Can God please erase that humongous lack of integrity on my part? Maybe fudge the bank camera so it wouldn't show me strutting into the bank lobby dressed as Sarah McIntyre? How about just turning the clock back twenty- four hours, so I wouldn't even have subjected myself to idiocy and illicit activities. Oh, and can God, also make sure I got both my jobs back?

"I have Pastor's number," I told Mother as I trudged out to see Dad, who was just as Mother had described...awake, but with eyes closed, and able only to grunt and squeeze my hand as I kissed him good-bye. I closed my eyes and tried to remember his face, capture it forever in my head, just in case, before I turned to leave the room for the final time.

Now, to confront Sarah.

I had a good mind to drag the poor little rich girl out of my bed. How had I imagined I could tolerate her snooty and deceptive attitude?

Of course, I wasn't going to enter the apartment by the balcony-window route I'd stooped to when I'd left. Who cared if she heard the alarm buzz declaring my escapade to visit my sick father? And I certainly hoped the Sleep Aid had given her no peaceful slumber, since her guilty conscience had better be on full throttle. I couldn't wait to hear her explain the photograph.

"So when, exactly, were you going to introduce me to your boyfriend, who *happens* to be my brother?" I'd ask her. "Was this a minor detail that slipped your mind, perhaps?" How about, "Are there any other insignificant particulars that might involve me that *maybe* you forgot to mention? Maybe a scheme to get rid of me in the near future? Or, to steal my identity and leave me to talk myself out of prison with the cops when they eventually figure out the bank fraud?

But, of course you'd be gone. Flaunting your wealth in some Caribbean beach, with my brother dangling on your tanned arm. With *my* identity!" So she could escape her uncle, she'd probably defend herself, those puppy- dog eyes welling up with tears.

The whole family reeked of plots.

What I couldn't wrap my brain around was why go through such lengths to trick her relations? I know they tried to get her killed, but surely there could have been a less roundabout way. It couldn't have been easy to get the fake IDs, for instance, yet she'd gone through the trouble. And the plane tickets under the assumed names? Just to trick me?

How did my brother fit into all this? *Walk it through slowly in your head, Brie.* You'll figure out why. But, better still, why not ask the psychopath herself?

❖ Chapter Thirty-Seven ❖

WHEN I NEARED MY MINI COOPER, a constant buzz was coming from inside it. As I took my car keys out, I considered the possibility of someone planting a bomb in my car. Would it blow apart when I opened the door? My eyes searched the interior of the car, and then I saw the cause of the continuous buzzing. Something flashed on and off on the passenger seat. It was my phone. Sarah! She'd probably discovered my sneaking out and wanted to vent her frustrations at me.

I answered the call without thinking twice, with a good mind to blow off some steam at her. *Who does she think she is?*

"Brianna?" The voice was certainly not Sarah's. It was a man's gravelly voice.

I glanced at the caller ID still on the face of the Samsung and saw it was Pastor Perry. *Trust him to catch me at a most unholy moment with expletives bursting out of me.*

"How are you?" he asked.

Fine, except I really would love to murder my roommate. "Been better. It's late."

"I know. I was praying for you and have a great burden in my heart, so I wanted to check how you've been," he went on.

I knew Pastor Perry felt a *burden* for many of the young adults, particularly the girls in our church. Mom said it was because his daughter had died, so every girl who was about her age when she'd passed on, seemed like a daughter to him.

"I meant to call. Lilly mentioned you had three dreams of me disappearing?"

He gave a low chuckle. "She's all ears, that one. I'll have to be careful what I say around her. I did have a dream of you disappearing but I was telling your mom about the three dreams Joseph had."

"Joseph with the multicolored cloak?"

"No, no. The other Joseph. Mary's husband and Jesus' adopted father. *He* had three dreams, too."

I'd heard Christmas stories, of course—how an angel visited Mary and told her she would be with child—the angel also visited Joseph in a dream, asking him to marry the expecting Mary. "I wasn't aware Joseph had that many dreams about Jesus. This is baby Jesus, right?"

"Right. Bear with me. I don't know what trouble awaits you, but I highlighted some Bible passages to help you."

"Sure." Why not have a Bible-study in the middle of the night, in the hospital parking lot to calm my nerves? I sat there in the dark in my car and waited. I really didn't want to be rude to this nice man. My mind was still on Sarah and Keith

Why couldn't Keith have just come to me? Share his problems, whatever they were, that he and Sarah were facing? I'm his sister. Was it so beneath Mr. Big-Shot Architect to ask his nobody sister for help?

"Brie, you there?" Pastor Perry asked.

"Yes, yes."

"Regarding Joseph's first dream, the Bible said this: 'Son of David, do not be afraid to take to you Mary your wife, for that which is conceived in her is of the Holy Spirit.' But, it was the second dream that I felt the Lord wanted me to share with you. May I read that?"

"Why not?" Preach on, Pastor.

"It comes from Matthew, chapter two. 'An angel of the Lord appeared to Joseph in a dream, saying, "Arise, take the young Child and His mother, flee to Egypt, and stay there until I bring you word; for Herod will seek the young Child to destroy Him."' So, God warned Joseph about the trouble awaiting him as Satan sought to kill Jesus, and shortly after they left Israel, Herod ordered all the baby boys under the age of two to be massacred."

"How's that related to me, exactly? I'm not about to massacre any babies." *Although, I could be persuaded to massacre one very spoiled heiress.*

"Of course, you're not going to hurt anyone. You have a kind heart, Brie. But, maybe it's a warning."

Like maybe someone was planning to massacre *me*? My heart pounded in my ears and suddenly the temperature in the car dropped. Was God dipping his head low below the clouds and trying to warn one Brie O'Mara? Miss Gullible, a la Naïve, herself?

"What was the third dream Joseph had?" I asked. Maybe there was something here.

"It's also from the Book of Matthew, chapter two. 'Now when Herod was dead, behold, an angel of the Lord appeared in a dream to Joseph in Egypt, saying, "Arise, take the young Child and His mother, and go to the land of Israel, for those who sought the young Child's life are dead.'

"'Then he arose, took the young Child and His mother, and came into the land of Israel. But when he heard that Archelaus was reigning over Judea instead of his father Herod, he was afraid to go there. And being *warned* by God in a *dream*, he turned aside into the region of Galilee.' So, Joseph was first told to return to Israel, then warned by God to go to Galilee."

"So, how is that related to me?" I asked again.

"God didn't fill me in with details. All He told me was to relate those passages to you. But, I know He loves you, Brie, and wants you safe. These are dark times for you, and it's not easy processing all that's happened to your father. And you must be supportive of your mother—she needs you now more than anything."

"Well, she has Keith."

"I probably shouldn't tell you now, but eventually you're going to find out."

The way he said this, my danger feelers tingled. "Find out, what?"

"Keith's going to be away for a few months, which means you're going to—"

"Wait! Where's he going?"

"I don't have the details, but he's been posted overseas, and he has to leave soon. Which means your mother—"

"Wait! Leave? How soon? When's Keith leaving?" Was he planning to leave with Sarah and me? That could be awkward.

"In a few days. Like I said, I don't have the details. I guess he didn't think it a big deal before, but now with your dad ill, it changes the picture, but he has already committed himself to this posting, and he doesn't want to ruin his career."

Of course, him being Mr. Ambitious.

My heart was beating so loudly I was sure Pastor Perry heard it. I found it hard to breathe, so I started the engine and brought the window down. "Do you know where exactly he's posted to?"

"'Fraid not."

"Thanks, Pastor. I appreciate it, really." I swallowed a lump in my throat. "But don't worry about me, okay? Dreams happen all the time.

Beside, God had good reasons to give Joseph those dream. But, you forget, I'm not important like Jesus. I doubt anyone's out to hurt me like that." And I clicked the phone off before he could say anything else.

❖ Chapter Thirty-Eight❖

BY THE TIME I REACHED my apartment's underground lot and parked, I was still seething with anger at Sarah for misleading me about her relationship with Keith. My heart pounded like an angry woodpecker, and I reminded myself to inhale deeply. Several possibilities played in my mind, and I kept telling myself not to speculate until I had all the facts. But, one reality stood out: Sarah and Keith had deceived me.

And how was Jackson involved in this? I reached under my seat, where I'd stuffed the envelope of paperwork Jim had compiled for me. I'd picked it up but hadn't had the chance to read through anything in there. I needed to catch my cool while I was still in the Mini Cooper. Make some sense while I still had my sanity.

I drew the rubber band-bound sheaf of papers out of the envelope and flipped through the dozen or so pages. Most were just articles about the Anderson and Partners, Attorneys-at-Law firm and a description of its services, which ran about a page.

A short list of paralegals and names of two junior partners and one senior partner, an Italian-sounding name.

A couple of newspaper write-ups in the *San Francisco Chronicle* and *San Jose Mercury* about the firm and its origin traced to West Virginia, the main partner having moved here four years back. I skimmed through everything in the dimness of the parking lot fluorescent light.

What caught my eye was the grainy picture of Jackson sitting on the edge of a desk. Jackson Anderson had a beefy face, a ruddy complexion, and a completely bald head. This was not the Jackson I had met at the bank! That Jackson had a full head of salt and pepper hair.

Instead of calming myself, this revelation further incensed me. Sarah must have hired that fake Jackson to fool the bank, knowing full well she'd never get the *real* Jackson to go along with her plan. This explained the brown bag that must have been filled with his pay. Where was the real Jackson? Maybe I could find him and spill the entire set-up to him. He'd know what to do.

I shoved the paperwork into the envelope and stuffed the package back under the driver's seat. Now it was time for Sarah to face the music, and for me to get some answers.

My steps made loud thuds on the carpeted hallway that led to my front door. Once I stepped inside, I turned off the alarm and switched on the living room lamp next to the door.

I half-expected Sarah to holler my room, complaining about the beep of the alarm. Still, she was probably sleeping like an infant, what with the margarita and pill combo, and I shouldn't have troubled myself by climbing that ledge and almost falling earlier. I'd left the front door of the vacant apartment next door unlocked. I'd take care of it after my serious talk with my split-tongued roommate. For now, nothing mattered but hearing what she had to say to justify her duplicity.

"Sarah!" I called her from outside the shut bedroom door. I pounded on it.

A rustle of papers startled me. The *Elle* magazine Sarah had flipped through earlier sat on the kitchen table, its pages fluttering. Where was the draft coming from? Had I left the window ajar? Come to think of it, the apartment felt more chilly than usual. An icy finger traced up my spine.

The sliding door that led to the balcony was open a crack. I could have sworn the slider had been shut tight when I'd left. I glanced at the microwave oven clock as I strode to close the sliding door. Two-thirteen, the digital clock read.

The alarm zone was set for every point of entry into the apartment, except my bedroom window and

Sarah's. I hadn't checked while coming in to see if someone had readjusted the alarm to bypass this particular slider.

Had Sarah left the apartment while I'd been gone? Why would she have done that?

I hadn't thought to check if her Jag was still parked in the usual lot. I recalled the red truck zooming past when I'd left. I wouldn't put it past Sarah to have planned another early-morning rendezvous with her secret boyfriend. Did my brother know about her two-timing ways? And how would this affect his relationship with her?

The hair behind my neck prickled more. Another thought hit me. An intruder could be in the apartment. Possibly the same one who'd tried to take Sarah out that time.

I stepped backwards two steps, and in the dim light of the living room's standing lamp, I saw the kitchen knife on the counter. Arming myself might not be a bad idea.

❖ Chapter Thirty-Nine ❖

I'D FLUNG THE LV backpack on the sofa when I'd stormed in and it felt miles away. If I could get to the bag, I could get my cell and call 911. I grabbed the knife and planted one foot in front of the other as I headed toward my LV—or rather, Sarah's LV, since mine was still in the bedroom. Yet Sarah hadn't responded, even with the ruckus I'd made. Was she in my room? Or was it someone else?

I glanced at the glass coffee table, but the note I'd stashed under the vase was gone. She must have found it—and what? Split for her nightly tryst with Mr. Red Truck, who might just be Keith? He did gravitate toward flashy-colored cars. Half of me hoped she was two-timing him.

I kept still and strained my ears. A rattling sound came from the bedroom Sarah was supposed to be sleeping in. If I dashed into the room, I could scare the intruder. But, with the racket I'd made, the intruder was probably gone. Unless he was waiting for me.

Where was Sarah? Nothing was making sense.

With giant leaps, I bounded toward the closed bedroom door and turned the knob, half-expecting it to be locked. Hoping it would be locked. But, it opened easily, and even in the darkness I could see Sarah on the bed, a hump bundled under the blanket, which could explain why she hadn't heard me. She slept with about a dozen pillows each night.

"Sarah!" I rushed toward her, yanked the blanket away, and shook her hard.

It wasn't Sarah on the bed. It wasn't anybody at all. It was just her blankets and her ridiculous number of pillows. I turned on the bedside lamp, the one with the frills that went around the bottom of the lamp shade.

The blankets and pillows were twisted together in a chaos, and blood splotches stained these. Blood was everywhere: on my lilac headboard, in patches on the carpet, and even on the wall above the headboard in a shape of a partial small handprint. Whose blood was this? The rusty smell of blood hit me.

I backed away from the bed and ran to the bathroom, my stomach twisted and nausea swelled up my throat.

"Sarah!" Still, no reply.

I rushed to Sarah's old bedroom, but the door was still locked. No one had gone in there, unless he or she had come in through that bedroom's window. The kitchen knife was still in my grip, and I determined to use its tip to break in. But I noticed something else.

The blade had faint smears; but now that I stared at it in the light, it looked suspicious. I brought it to my nose. Blood. I dropped it by my feet. Was the knife the murder weapon?

Who'd done this? Her uncle? His conspirators? Whoever did this must have gotten into our apartment through the balcony sliding door. Maybe even through Mrs. Mott's empty apartment. And I'd left that front door open! If I'd been here I might have heard him, them, stopped whoever they were. We must have been watched all this while.

But, where was Sarah? Was she hurt, or had something worse happened? The amount of blood I'd witnessed made me shudder.

Then it occurred to me. If I'd been home I, too, could have been hurt, or killed. And I'd slipped her those sleeping pills. She'd been helpless, and I was to blame.

Sarah's LV still lay on the sofa where I'd dumped it.

I made a dash for it and searched for my cell phone. I would call Jim, ask him what to do. He'd have friends who could help. But, what if the cops thought I was in on this heinous crime? Worse, what if they believed I'd gotten rid of Sarah to get my hands on her money, just as she'd joked earlier?

I found Sarah's iPhone, but it was still locked. Useless. My hands groped about the bag, and finally in frustration I dumped the entire contents of her bag onto the sofa. Everything came flying out as I jerked the LV upside-down. Everything but my phone. I'd left it in the Mini Cooper in my fury to confront Sarah!

Then, it hit me. My fingerprints. On the knife. On the balcony. On the window sill. On the sliding door. And in Mrs. Mott's vacant apartment next door. which I'd left unlocked so I could use it again to return via the ledge. I'd have to explain everything. Would the cops believe me? What if I couldn't reach Jim? I'd heard about cops pinning the crime on the most convenient suspect. And I'd have given them motive,--ninety-nine million dollars' worth of motive--,the most powerful weapon they could use against me.

I could call Jackson. Not the fake one who'd called and left a number with my mom, all a ploy to take my guard down. The real Jackson, the one whose office I'd contacted using the business card from Sarah's drawer. He'd know what to do, how to help me. What if he thought I was guilty, too? He wasn't going to be pleased Sarah and I had tricked the bank. Tricked him. Committed a crime. But, I was no murderer. I'd never even had a traffic ticket.

I couldn't call Dad. Mom? She was already stressed by my father's condition, although she and the nurses at Palo Alto Hospital could surely give me an alibi. But, when had this vicious slaying at my apartment taken place? Right after I'd left? Or before? Then I'd remembered I'd heard it! That crash

I'd mistaken for Sarah dropping something—it could have been her struggling? And I hadn't even helped her.

I would call Keith. He'd be devastated. He'd want to know. Regardless of the reason for them deceiving me, it couldn't possibly be anything close to murder. Keith and I had grown up together, swinging on the rubber tubing attached to the old oak tree and playing hide-and-seek in our backyard. My apartment didn't have a landline, so I'd have to retrieve my cell from the Mini Cooper to contact anyone.

I took out Sarah's phone, and tried different combinations: her birthday, her favorite pet's name that she said died two years back, our zip code. No success.

What was her password?

I snatched a rag from a kitchen drawer and started wiping surfaces—the sliding door, the balcony. I ran to old Mrs. Mott's vacant apartment and used the rag to wipe my prints off places I'd touched. But, what if I also wiped off any evidence of the intruder? I took a deep breath and backed away toward Mrs. Mott's front door, locked it, and rushed to my car. I had Sarah's LV with me, in addition to my own bag, which I'd found by the foot of my bed.

Had the intruder killed Sarah, thinking she was me? He, or they, must have noticed my LV. Maybe even looked inside it. And my yellow duffel by the foot of the bed—that, too, could have fooled them.

As I gathered my wits in my car in that empty garage I thought of what I'd say to Keith. A high-powered vehicle revved its engine as it sped down the street. My heart skipped several beats. Every sound seemed magnified. The red truck popped into my head.

I resolved it was perhaps wisest to call Jackson first. He'd known Sarah the longest. He cared for her. He was connected to people in law enforcement. He, of all people, could help me— prove I was innocent, in case the cops insisted on having someone in custody quickly. *I should try his cell.* Not even a workaholic attorney would be at his office at four in the morning, but he might sleep with his phone on, right by his bedside table, as I'd seen in those detective shows.

Fingers trembling, I punched the private number Jackson had passed my mom.

His number rang twice, then went dead. I tried it again. I couldn't get through. On a third try, a female voice answered. "The number you've dialed is no longer in service. Please check the number and try again."

What?

The alternative was his office number. No decent legal office on the Pacific coast would stay open at this hour, but I keyed in the office contact on Jackson's card anyway.

After two rings, a man's voice answered. I

almost said, "Mr. Anderson!" but the voice was a recording—a strange one, too.

"If you are calling to reach the Jackson Anderson, Attorney Services, please note that due to the recent situation, all clients of the late Mr. Jackson Anderson have been re-routed to his associate and trusted senior partner, Mr. Antonio Ghirardellio. Please leave your name, number, and best time to reach you. Otherwise, all existing clients will be contacted in due process. Thank you for your understanding during this difficult time."

I hung up the phone, hardly believing my ears.

The late Mr. Jackson Anderson? Who was the imposter I'd seen at the bank? He might not *just* have been a fake Jackson; could he have been involved in the real Jackson's demise? Sarah surely must not have known. That brown bag, which I presumed must have contained cash, she'd passed him must just have been payment for services at the bank. Right? Or was it for something else, too?

My hope of obtaining Jackson's help to clear my name vanished. Was his death, if indeed that was the "recent situation," related to Sarah's disappearance? Had she died? A deal turned sour, double-crossed by the body-double Jackson? It was possible Sarah was kidnapped for ransom, which meant a demand was forthcoming. But what if no ransom note came? And what about all that blood? If the intruders had meant her to be done away, where did that leave me? My fingers gripping the cell phone went numb and I realized I'd grasped it too tightly.

The world around me swirled like a cesspool. I'd hardly grabbed any dinner, and lack of sleep fuzzed my thinking. A sound out on the street jerked me out of my despair, and I sucked in a sharp breath that caught in my throat. Sirens. Police cars, or a fire engine? Someone might have reported Sarah's tragedy. Someone could be watching the apartment and wanting to place the entire blame on me. They must have noticed I'd returned. But why pin it on me?

Think. Think. Think logically, I chided myself.

But my hands kept trembling, and I clasped the steering wheel in a vain attempt to steady my nerves. I couldn't control my breathing. Stay calm. Focus. Think one step at a time.

If the person reported me, that meant he wanted me framed, which meant he must want something I have, something I'd lose if caught with a crime. I thought about what I'd said to Pastor Perry. I did have something enough for me to be a target for evil.

The will! The inheritance was only Sarah's if she was a law-abiding citizen. Maybe that clause also transferred to the person to whom she passed the inheritance. The people who knew about our scheme were Sarah, myself, the fake Jackson, possibly Keith, and possibly her Uncle Stu. Maybe Stu found out, somehow. The siren grew loud, but just as I scrambled to start my car and zoom off, the scream of the siren dissipated into the night as if the vehicle had turned a corner.

I needed to think without the noise blaring into my head. Fingers fumbling, I snatched the envelope Jim had passed me from under my seat and stuffed it into my LV. I rushed back up to the apartment, shut the front door, and turned the alarm on. *Breathe slowly*. I waited in the dark—for what I didn't know. I was alone.

If I could get into Sarah's phone, I might find something that could help me. The password must have been something easy for her to remember, obvious to her but to no one else. Her big secret? R-E-D-T-R-U-C-K. I keyed the words in. Nothing happened.

I tried my luck once more—not that my luck could be depended upon these days. Keith's name. Didn't work either. Then I tried K-E-I-T-H-1-9-8-3—the year Keith had been born. The iPhone burst into life, screen flashing into a brilliant firework, then welcoming me. Or rather, Sarah.

My finger scrolled down the recent calls she'd made. No names were linked to any of the numbers. I saw she'd called Keith that very afternoon. Several times. I recognized his number. One must have been right after our Fremont Bank affair. So, he knew. Why else would she have called right after, as if she was updating him? Was he the mastermind? My own brother? If Jackson's death was not an accident, perhaps my brother was involved, too.

❖ Chapter Forty❖

IF I COULD LOCATE that small green book Sarah had with all those name cards, I might also find who her contacts had been. Plus, her brother's frequent haunts were in it. Todd might be able to help me if I struck a deal with him, especially since he was after Sarah's share. Help me prove that Sarah was behind this crime and that I had nothing to do with what had happened here earlier, and he could have double portion. But where was Todd?

Those scraps Sarah had stuffed in her LV might hold some clues as to what had happened. I dumped her bag's contents onto the sofa again and sifted through the mountain of receipts, bills and purchase invoices. The receipts didn't amount to anything significant except confirmation of what I already knew: she was a heavy shopper.

Every name brand was probably represented in the pile. If I sold all her belongings, I could probably make a million bucks.

But, where were these items she'd purchased? To think I was so close to having ninety-nine million to my name and couldn't get to it unless I wanted to risk spending my life behind bars, or worse, the gas chamber. That was the death penalty of California for first degree murder.

Her closet didn't hold that much by way of clothes, or shoes, or bags. She might have forwarded them to the London address, the one she'd mentioned briefly. What about the safe in her room? She claimed to have cleaned all the stock certificates out of it, but in any case, I couldn't open it. I paged through the receipts again. In one of them I saw a name—a warehouse bill from Home Storage, "A place for your treasured belongings" the subtitle read. Address: 375, Portland Lane, Menlo Park. And the unit number, 410.

I vaguely remembered Portland Lane. It wasn't in the industrial part of town where most of the self-storage buildings were located, and Atherton hardly had a commercial section. Home Storage must be an expensive alternative to the normal storage places. She must have stashed her valuables there.

Where had she hidden the key to the warehouse? Was she planning to return to the Bay Area to collect her items? Or was Keith to take care of the nitty-gritty for her? Things hadn't added up yet. If I called Mom she might know Keith's scheduled move to Europe.

But first, I had to locate that storage key. The thought of going into Sarah's bedroom made my stomach churn. The room itself would remind me of her—her expensive Hanae-somebody perfume, the scent of her vanilla shampoo, her smell of betrayal—but if I wanted to save myself, I'd need to find some other information to clear my name.

It was already four-thirty. The flight to Mexico City was supposed to be at noon. Sarah's K twin friends were to collect my Mini Cooper and clear out the furniture soon after we were supposed to have left the apartment at ten.

Sarah had never confirmed what she was planning to do with her green Jaguar Coupe. I'd actually brought it up and she'd given me vague answers. Gift it to Keith, perhaps? The Jag would fetch quite a sum. It might be her sick idea of a parting present for him, her way of saying sorry if she never meant to see him again.

If I could get the paperwork, maybe I could sell the Jag. But what car dealer was open at this hour, anyway? I wondered about the red truck. Had Keith been driving it? He was always partial to hot colors. Yellow. Red. Or, was it Sarah's second boyfriend? I could call Keith—confront him, tell him I'd seen him in a red truck. Then I could at least know what I was dealing with.

Calmer, I was able to remember the spare screwdriver in the kitchen drawer. We'd always used it to pop the doorknob mechanism open when we'd accidentally locked our bathroom doors from the wrong side. I inhaled deeply and slowly made my way to Sarah's bedroom. The safe was still in the closet that smelled of her perfume. The fragrance, a soft lilac and vanilla scent, still lingered in there. The safe sat in the back, where her clothes had once hung.

The door was slightly ajar, and when I tugged it open, I saw the safe was empty. At least a few million dollars' worth of stock certificates were gone. They could either be on route to London, or Sarah might have deposited them in the warehouse.

If I took them and sold them, could the cops trace everything back to me? I was eighteen and had never even bought stocks. I didn't know the ins and outs of the stock exchange rules.

A buzz in the LV on my shoulder jolted me. Someone had texted or left a message on one of the cell phones. Which, I couldn't tell. I went to Sarah's drawers first to look for anything that could throw light on my dire situation. Nothing. Everything was already packed in her suitcases.

Perhaps the key to the warehouse was in her luggage, too—in one of her ridiculous, old-fashioned suitcases I'd laughed at the suitcases when she'd rolled them into the apartment on Mrs. Mott's dolly that day she'd moved in.

"These aren't suitcases," I'd teased her that evening. "Who uses these carriage chests with leather bindings and heavy buckles, nowadays? You need a footman."

Those were some of the most expensive suitcases, she'd boasted—vintage Louis Vuitton that only the best auctioneers could get a hold of, since they had been discontinued decades ago. The cases bore leather hand- stitching all around to reinforce the edges and sold for about ten thousand apiece.

I could sell her antique suitcases, if I got desperate. Of course, lugging them around would be conspicuous for they didn't even have wheels.

For now, I needed to see what loot lay inside them. After staring at the brown checkered design for too many precious minutes, I took a deep breath and heaved both cases to the living room.

As I fiddled with the locks I wondered how the perpetrator would have carried Sarah's body out of the apartment. Slung over a shoulder like a worn carpet, or dragged by the arms? I hadn't noticed the hallway carpet smeared with anything that resembled blood. I walked back to the scene of the crime and looked about.

The rug in front of my bed was missing! It was only a four-by-six but it was big enough to roll a person in. I stared at the patch where the rug used to sit. My dream came back to me. What if the rug was meant for *my* body?

I went to the front door and peered through the peephole. At this hour, it was unlikely any of the neighbors down this hallway would be up. The apartment didn't even have security cameras I could depend on to clear my name. And, where were those keys for the suitcases? I thought to pick the locks of the bags open with the screwdriver, but I might have need for them intact. They were impossible to pry without breaking the entire lock mechanism.

I had tarried too long. The criminals could return. Especially if they found they'd done away with the wrong girl.

❖ Chapter Forty-One❖

HURRIEDLY, I OPTED for the only choice I had. Her car keys were exactly where she always kept them— in a kitchen drawer still filled with silverware that was now meant for Mr. Yamamoto's next tenants. I gathered my luggage together with Sarah's things and took the four suitcases to her Jag.

After two trips to get all the bags squeezed into the back, I huddled in the driver's seat, grabbed her cell phone, and checked the newest message. Who'd have texted her at this unearthly hour?

"Ready? Wait 4 U near car. ETA 5. C ya," the text read.

It was from Keith's number.

Was that five as in five minutes? Or at five o'clock? I glanced at the time on my phone: 4:37. Was he in the garage already? Spying on me struggling with all those suitcases, wondering what I was up to? But the text meant he expected Sarah to meet him. Something had gone awfully awry for him, too. If I went to him and begged him to help would he forget our differences, and be my alibi? But could I trust a snake?

In our original plan, Sarah and I weren't supposed to leave till nine thirty. She'd stressed that was the earliest we could scoot out of the apartment. San Francisco Airport was only twenty minutes away, and that would have given us more than a couple of hours to check in and seat ourselves comfortably in our Air Mexicano flight to Mexico City.

It was certainly possible that Sarah had been planning to ditch me. Perhaps I wasn't even meant to be on that flight because she had known all along that a hit- man was scheduled to do me in.

It was also possible that she was to leave with Keith. And I was not supposed to be in the picture because I was supposed to be dead. Dead. She wanted me *dead*? I pressed the heels of my palms deep into my eye sockets. *Stop wasting time! Stop being so stupid!*

I stared at the two airline tickets in my hand and turned them over to inspect them. Were these fake? If I tried to use the "Sienna Smith" name would I trigger the alarm? Only one way to find out.

That was when I resolved my future. I would gather my things, just as previously planned by Sarah, and make my getaway. I would run away, at least for a while. Take that flight to Mexico City at noon and think things through once I was airborne. Figure out who I could call for help. Who could I trust?

My phone buzzed, and I almost suffered a seizure from it. My turn to get a text this early. What if it was Keith demanding I explain myself as he watched me like a vulture eyeing its dying prey from a far corner in the underground lot? Or like a cobra waiting to strike: an analogy Sarah had used to describe her uncle earlier. I glanced about but noticed no movement. Only other parked cars. Every vehicle seemed vacant. The Jag's digital clock said four-fifty.

Something about my older brother had made me uneasy when I'd met him at the hospital. His skimming around the edges of my questions, as if he kept a dark secret. I'd never imagined, of course, it would involve his girlfriend. His dead girlfriend, maybe. And me.

He might have orchestrated the entire plot, right up to the bank scheme. Planned for Sarah to move in with me. Keith knew I had a clean record, never traveled— something I always bemoaned to him since he'd made so many European trips—and I had no passport. Nobody would ever suspect Keith was on the sidelines.

If Sarah planned to be me and not include me in the final take, that could only mean one thing, one horrible thing I couldn't bear to contemplate. I wiped my eyes with my sleeves. I'd thought she was my friend. Maybe even my best friend. But, what if she'd planned for me to get killed instead? All along?

She must have been driven to despair. To keep herself free from her uncle—whom she claimed wouldn't give her any peace until he got his hand on some of her money—and to make him think she was gone for good.

She must have wanted to make it look as if I'd murdered her.

She must have hired some thug to break in and hurt me while I lay asleep. Maybe the same thug who'd broken in that first time. That, too, could have been a ruse.

That could explain why she hadn't wanted the authorities alerted in any way—had insisted upon it, even though she'd seemed scared stiff. This could also explain why the thug never actually hurt her—just some scratches on her forehead, which could have been self- inflicted.

If her uncle, or her brother, was deceived into thinking she was dead, or at least deemed dead, what with all that blood found in the bedroom, either one might not persist in searching for Sarah. Instead, searching for Brianna O'Mara might occupy their waking hours—the girl who'd conned Sarah into switching identities with her and then done her in and escaped with the loot.

They would search, but probably never find "Brie O'Mara" because once she was out of the USA and living in the Bahamas or some remote country with lax laws, she could access the inheritance and they might never locate her amongst Earth's seven billion population. They could pass pictures of Brie around and Sarah could go back to looking like herself.

To make more sense of what had gone on, I continued to theorize.

Posed as someone else, Sarah was to escape with Keith, or another bf, and people would think I had committed those atrocities; Brie O'Mara had killed her roommate, after fooling her into bequeathing her fortune, just so she could live out her own dreams. The cops wouldn't be looking for a dead Brianna O'Mara but a criminal.

The horror hit me once again. Sarah wasn't supposed to be mutilated. I was. The longer I sat there staring into the steering wheel, the more convinced I became. The missing dead body should have been mine, I was certain of it. Even if I couldn't prove it.

Yet, Sarah had gone through elaborate details to get the fake credentials for me. And, how was she going to fool the cops? Make them think it was her? Especially if my blood was splattered all over the bedroom?

Then, I recalled how she had gone to the hospital or the doctor's. She'd come home with a patch on her arm and dismissed it as a blood test she had to take. What if she'd been having her blood drawn? Blood meant to be used to trick the cops?

Two weeks was the limit for blood banks before the cells began to break down, my father had explained once a long time ago. Tests for falling nitric oxide levels could determine how old blood was but within a fortnight the blood stayed fresh. It was only a few days ago that she'd had her blood drawn. The intruders could have kept the blood as good as new for her till the night of the crime. Till they had to sprinkle her blood on my bed. Splatter it.

That refrigerated safe!

What if, she'd stored the blood in it? The blood could be used to fool the authorities. She'd been upset when she couldn't have my bed dismantled. And when I'd offered my bed she was reluctant to sleep in my room. I'd thought it was because she was being thoughtful. But, what if, it was because she was afraid the blood was not going to stay acceptable out of the refrigerated safe for an hour or so?

Again my heart couldn't accept this. It couldn't be.

And what about DNA? Hair evidence that would have shown it was mine if I were killed? Easy— they'd just have to be thorough like when they broke in the first time. They could have easily planted Sarah's hair and skin cells. And besides, we visited each other's rooms.

Fingerprints? Of course, now my fingerprints were even on the knife. And the walls outside, over the ledge, if the cops ever looked there.

What had gone wrong that had made the hit man mistake Sarah for me? The note on the table had been missing. Could my message for Sarah have misled them?

At this point, I couldn't imagine this being a one- person job. Perhaps once in, and reading the note, they had assumed Sarah was in her bedroom, and having checked that door was locked, had gone to my bedroom, believing Brianna O'Mara was sleeping in her own bed, with her yellow duffel by the side of the bedside table, and her LV with all her personal belongings next to it. That alcohol-sleeping pill combo before she'd crashed on my bed must have knocked her out.

After minutely detailing the plot, she must have not realized the thugs would not think to check it was me first before their slaughter. Sarah must have slipped up in this—perhaps her fatigue and the stress contributed to this mistake. The fact that I had her phone further testified to this. She'd never bothered to tell anyone she'd had to sleep in my room. Maybe they'd even GPS'd her phone to confirm she was not in that bedroom.

I peeked at the text on my cell. I recognized the number, even though I hadn't added it to my contact list and probably never would, for I needed to excommunicate myself from my past.

The text read: "Know u r an early bird, so didn't think u'd mind. Glad u visited yr dad." Pastor Perry.

Maybe I should respond to Pastor Perry. Perry Mason, I should call him. He'd dreamed of me disappearing. And then, those warnings for me from

God? If I had heeded the warnings from my own bizarre nightmares, would I be in this mess? I wanted to tell him the dung I'd dug myself into. But, I couldn't justify all I'd done. He couldn't save me. I clung to the passages he'd shared about God warning Joseph to flee Egypt. Was it possible God wanted me to flee? If I told Pastor Perry, would he report me?

Confidentiality obligations bound priests on TV, but I couldn't say if this was fact or fiction. If I had time, I could research, but it was already 4:56.

"ETA 5," Keith had texted.

The sound of traffic had increased on the street in front of my apartment. Life was stirring up around me.

And Keith could be driving up any second.

My life, however, seemed headed toward a dead dream. Nobody to turn to. Jim wasn't answering my calls. Pete, too, seemed distant. I was completely on my own— ironically, something I'd yearned for since the day I'd tossed my graduation hat with its golden tassels high in the sky after the celebration.

I couldn't possibly go to my parents—drag them into this mire, put them through this shame, and see their disappointment. I couldn't live with myself. If what I had left could qualify as life.

Besides, my parents have enough troubles of their own.

If I didn't leave soon Keith would catch me here.

I'd locked and armed the alarm for the apartment.

That would buy me time before he found Sarah had not kept her appointment. If he loved her, he might panic, and it sounded like he was smitten by her. Maybe he suspected she was two-timing him with the red truck guy, whoever he was

Did Sarah plan to just rendezvous with Keith one last time before she ditched him? He could have been too controlling. Maybe she realized he was lured to her money. It felt like everything hitched on that Red Truck Guy. Maybe she wanted to make him believe she had scooted off to Hawaii as she'd wanted the cops to believe, too. So to what extent was Keith in on the scheme? And if he was in it for the money and meant to frame me, he might not be inclined to call the cops, lest he became a suspect.

As long as Keith didn't break down the apartment door I would have time to get away. Unless she'd given him a spare key.

Plan carefully, Brie. Don't be stupid again.

I would text the K twins from Sarah's phone, tell them there was a slight delay, that they should come the next day, instead of this morning. When they discovered the bloodstained bedroom, I would be in Mexico.

For now, I would go to a secluded spot and dig through Sarah's suitcases. The key to the warehouse had to be in there. If I hurried I could get to the warehouse undetected. I would dress like Sarah, put on that fitted Burberry jacket of hers, so the warehouse camera would think it was her if the cops got a hold of the images. I would browse through her possessions there that might throw some light on the situation. Find that small green book with the name cards and all of Todd's whereabouts.

Worst case, I might get a hold of some money in the storage place, or from the suitcases. I would need hard cash once I left the States. Since Sarah believed in only using cash, I was banking on the hope her luggage would hold stacks enough for me to survive on.

The cops would be watching the banks, once they thought Sarah had been murdered and they uncovered the imposter scam we committed. I had no clue how to make withdrawals from the account that was now legally mine, assuming Sarah was gone forever.

Her contact, Brian Sussman, might also be under the authorities' radar. Who knew h o w h e m i g h t b e connected? But, with some funds, I could hire a private investigator to get in touch with him secretly. Provided he existed.

For now, I trusted no one, would speak to no one. After all, how did I even know the dark brown follicle found in Sarah's room on the night of the break-in hadn't been planted by Jim? Money, Sarah said, could buy people. Had Sarah bought him, too? It could explain his refusal to return my messages and calls. But, surely, Pete wouldn't have stooped so low. I brushed the back of my hand over my eyes.

The news would report the story of Sarah's disappearance and possible murder. It might even make it to the breaking news section on CNN's homepage. When, and if, her body would turn up, I couldn't tell. As long as she remained missing, the prosecution did not have a case against me, and I still stood to be her beneficiary...provided I never got caught and no one killed me.

Forget a normal life. Forget dreams of ever getting into a New York City college. Forget acting and debuting on Broadway. Forget Drew. All my dead dreams. The question that would haunt me every waking moment from this day forth would be: Will they ever find Sarah?

Half of me hoped so; the other half wasn't so sure. Was it better to run away indefinitely and never get caught? Or, should I turn myself in and confess to the authorities my share of the crime?

I could disappear into the faceless crowd. As long as Sarah was never found, what could they really pin on me? If I hid, I could live as a person free from the bounds of prison. If the guilt that plagued me was not considered a chain in itself.

To Be continued in Book 2. Out Mid 2014.

Watch out for Book 2 coming out summer 2014. Sign up for the newsletter to get updates and contest information.

If you have enjoyed this book please leave your short review on Amazon, BN.com or your e-retailer, and leave your comments @ http:www.emmaright.com

Follow Emma Right's blog on homeschooling, young adult and children's books, self-publishing, contests and updates and more: @EmmaRight.com/Blog

Other Books By Emma Right

KEEPER OF REIGN BOOK 1 (Reign Fantasy series) for readers 10-16.

Get your copy of **KEEPER OF REIGN** at your favorite retailer.

Summary of **Keeper of Reign Book 1**:

Books written in blood. Most are lost, their Keepers with them. A curse that befell a people. A Kingdom with no King. Life couldn't get more harrowing for the Elfies, a blend of Elves and Fairies. Or for sixteen-year-old Jules Blaze. Or could it? For Jules, the heir of a Keeper, no less, suspects his family hides a forgotten secret. It was bad enough that his people, the Elfies of Reign, triggered a curse which reduced the entire inhabitants to a mere inch centuries ago. All because of one Keeper who failed his purpose. Even the King's Ancient Books, did not help ward off that anathema.

Now, Gehzurolle, the evil lord, and his armies of Scorpents, seem bent on destroying Jules and his family. Why? Gehzurolle's agents hunt for Jules as he journeys into enemy land to find the truth. Truth that could save him and his family, and possibly even reverse the age- long curse. Provided Jules doesn't get himself killed first.

To see the world of Reign visit Pinterest.com/emmaright and see images of the Incredible world of Reign and Characters from the Kingdom of Reign, as well as book awards and possible future covers from the series.

Prisoner of Reign, Book 2 of the Reign Fantasy series will be out 2014

Visit Emma at http://www.emmaright.com or

Facebook at Emma Right Author

Twitter follow @emmbeliever

Emma Right Books:

The Princesses of Chadwick Castle Mystery series for girls

Beautiful Ballerina series

Beautiful Ballerina Gift Book

Keeper of Reign, Book 1,pre-teen and teen fantasy

Prisoner of Reign, Book 2, pre-teen and teen fantasy

Dead Dreams, a young adult psychological thriller

 ❖ ❖ ❖

About the Author

Award Winning and Best Seller author, Emma Right, is a happy wife and Christian homeschool mother of five living in the Pacific West Coast of the USA. Besides running a busy home, and looking after their five pets, which includes two cats, two bunnies and a Long-haired Dachshund, she also writes stories for her children. When she doesn't have her nose in a book, she is telling her kids to get theirs in one.

Emma worked as a copywriter for two major advertising agencies and won several awards, including the prestigious Clio Award for her ads, before she settled down to have children. Emma Right is currently features in Authors' Network latest book, *50 Great Authors You Should be Reading*. She can be contacted through her website at http://www.emmaright.com/

❖ ❖ ❖